I0682613

Around the Block
On Parnell Square

Around the Block Writers Collaborative

Around the block on Dublin's Parnell Square is The Charles Stewart Guesthouse, named in honor of the patriot Charles Stewart Parnell and also the birthplace of Oliver St. John Gogarty, a poet friend of James Joyce. Here in March of 2012, nine Americans gathered for a week of writing that was in part inspired by the short story collection, *Finbar's Hotel* by Dermot Bolger and six other Irish authors.

We, too, began with our setting: that lovely, historical Georgian home adapted and expanded into a guesthouse on Dublin's north side. Writing independently, we developed nine fictional characters to inhabit those unique, quirky spaces and then invented their life stories during our daily workshops. *Around the Block on Parnell Square* is purely the work of our imaginations, and we are grateful to Helen and her fine staff at The Charles Stewart for creating an atmosphere that encouraged our creative spirits to roam those carpeted halls and Dublin's cobblestoned streets with complete abandon.

Contents

Fallen angels and plates of beans

Kathleen Worrell

That morning at the Charles Stewart Guesthouse, Moira Kelley served 80 poached eggs, 6 scrambled, 172 broiled tomato halves, 150 pieces of bacon, 12 sausages, and 100 pieces of toast, browned in the broiler on one side, pallid on the other. And beans. Some days it makes her homesick for her Granny's home-made beans, not the bland tinned ones, but with slivers of onion and shreds of bacon. Her Granny's oat cakes are not limp white rags but dense, brown, and chewy.

But Moira fled those breakfasts, fled all of Howth and its fishing processing plants as soon as she graduated high school. Thirty minutes from Dublin, Howth seems at the ends of the earth. Now she serves Irish breakfasts to the hotel's guests, cleans their rooms, makes their beds fresh, and scours their tubs and sinks. She admires the women's clothing and inhales the scent of their shampoos and perfumes. There is so much to learn in Dublin.

The fan in her minute bathroom is so loud that Moira feels its vibration tremble right down to her toenails which are a newly applied shade of rose. She inspects her pale face in the mirror, bemoaning once again the dull light that yellows her complexion.

It is such a tiny bathroom, and Moira is not a tiny girl. The shower is like an upright coffin and the sink no bigger than a cereal bowl. Her friend Ioana, over whom Moira towers, would find the bathroom spacious. However, it is blissfully hers; no sharing with sisters, brothers, or parents. Number B, as she calls it, is the only bedroom in the basement area and next to the kitchen. Ioana's room is a former coat closet turned into a living space. Since Ioana is barely 4-feet tall, it fits perfectly.

Moira sits on her single bed with its board hard mattress, heavy blankets and dense pillows with a sigh. A large wooden wardrobe takes up half the room and holds all her belongings. Dark blue drapes give the illusion of a view beyond, but when open, reveal only a 6-inch high window. It is the basement, after all.

Once her shift is over, out she goes, rain, drizzle, sun, to walk the streets and negotiate the shops down on Nassau Street. Or she walks in St. Stephen's Green, always observing the city girls to see what they are wearing, envious at their confidence.

At the Charles Stewart, the various guests are mostly too old to be of much interest, like the short-haired man with glasses who always wears a dress shirt and carries a notebook he studies over his breakfast. He says he is searching for his Irish roots. Or the woman with the flat American accent built like a ship leaving Dublin Bay. No, not very interesting, the older ones.

Moira yearns to learn more about Mo with the bleached Mohawk or the birdlike one with the red streak in her hair and tons of earrings; Bridget her name is. Moira shudders to think of all the piercings. Does it hurt, getting pierced? And Bridget has a tattoo at the base of her neck. Surely those needles were painful too.

There are a group of Americans doing a writing class at the Charles Stewart. They always seem to be having such a good time. One of the husbands inquired after the local farmer's market, and she steered him the right direction. Later, she saw him arranging trays of sliced vegetables, cheese, meats, and good Irish wheat bread to take into the others. It amazes her that a man could be that capable in the kitchen. At home, it is only the women who cook while the men sit at the table, impatient for their food. If she is lucky, someday she might find herself a man who likes to cook and they can work in the kitchen together. Ah, it is a dream, but a pleasant one.

It was Ioana the Romanian who befriended her first, emerging from the closet off the kitchen where she ironed sheets and pillow cases for the guest rooms. So short she only comes to Moira's shoulder, Ioana looks about Dublin with squinty eyes, easily angered when she thinks the Irish are looking down on her foreignness. Ioana came to work at the Irish Film Festival but, to her despair, was rejected and reduced to working at the Charles Stewart. Moira knows what loneliness is like in the city and remembers how city people considered her provincial for being from Howth.

For that reason, she accepts Ioana's offer to go to a pub that Friday night where the music and crowds of young men brighten your mood. She tries her first vodka, and oh it is harsh going down, not at all like the Guinness. Ioana doesn't seem to mind the taste in the least.

The Temple Bar is crowded for a week night, throngs of tourists and college students on holiday crowd around the bar. At one table Moira spots the group of American writers drinking beer and clapping to the music. She is envious of their camaraderie.

Nearby are the woman Mo and a lady called Posey who always wears a pink leather mini skirt, black tights and spiky boots and carries a floral bag big enough to hold six pints of beer. Mo is a nanny for several "spoiled rotten brats" as she calls them, but she has a natural cheerfulness to her. Posey Mulvane always seems to be in a state of depression, given to deep sighs. Once, Moira caught her wandering the hallways of the Charles Stewart as if in a trance.

The band plays what is expected, *Galway Girl* and *Danny Boy* and *Will Ye Go Lassie Go*. Moira watches this man and that, but cannot elicit any interest from the college students. It is just as well, she confides to Ioana, who is drinking two vodkas to her one and is beginning to mutter about the injustice of the Irish film world once again.

"Oh, look, Ioana, isn't that Harold from the hotel? I'm sure it is." The thought brings rosy hue to her pale complexion. Moira fetches Harold's coffee each day to where he presides over the front desk. Just this morning he said softly, *Thanks, luv.*

Harold is from Holland and possesses soft blond hair cut so it forms a peak from forehead to back of skull, a new fashion among young working men in Dublin. His blue eyes are round, wide and innocent, framed by lovely dark lashes that Moira wishes were her own. He is popular with the guests for he always answers all questions with a smile and accuracy. The female guests flush with pleasure as he chats them up.

Ioana swivels narrow eyes in his direction, studies him and the blonde companion who is leaning across the table toward him, features angry, desperate, both hands on the tabletop as if about to rise. Moira feels her mood deflate. Who is the woman? Why is she upset with Harold? The back of her blue sweater seems to tremble as she turns and leaves Harold behind.

"Phooey. You do better than that, Moira. You can't trust a man who says he's from Holland. Double phooey. You can't trust a man, period."

Before Moira can answer, Ioana stands up, wavers against the table, and then resolutely marches out to the sidewalk, one hand like a claw about Moira's wrist, dragging her along like a reluctant child.

The next morning finds Moira in a pitiable shape. Never again, she murmurs the mantra, never again. Only pale beer. She soaks the redness from her eyes, reduces the pallor with her hard earned new cosmetics from LUSH, widens and brightens her gaze with liner, mascara, and eye shadow. Never, never, never again.

The clatter of the kitchen almost does her in as the cook bangs pans on the stove for frying eggs and pots of simmering water for poached ones. Moira opens tins of pork and beans and nearly gags as she pours them into a stock pot to heat. Then she sets to work slicing tomatoes for broiling.

She is glad to see that Ioana looks worse than she does, sitting before her work, the steam from the iron beading on her chin, her eyelids drooping like shades pulled against the sun. Someone drops a spoon and both of them flinch. Never again.

Moira's headache has diminished when the guests begin to settle at their tables. She carries out plate after plate filled with bacon, sausage, eggs, beans, and tomatoes. The one Harold refers to as *that Heavenly Warrior fellow* from Room 403 beckons to her. No bacon or eggs for him. No vodka either, she bets. Just the fruit and oak cakes and some strange tea he brings with him.

He is one of the old ones, but Moira has to admire his slender tan fingers, his firm muscled arms, the well-toned body, and mass of long hair like those heroes on the covers of romance novels. She imagines he is tanned all over; the thought brings a tiny smile to her lips, and he nods, giving her one in return.

He might think she is too young for the likes of him, too hefty of thigh and plump about the shoulders. But one never knows, do they? What is too young and what is too old? It gives spice to life. Today will be cinnamon and sugar, she decides, and goes back to the kitchen to prepare Harold from Holland a special plate of toast to eat along with his coffee.

Harold is preoccupied this morning, a frown forming a crease between those lovely blue eyes. *You're a luv*, he says, when he sees the toast. *I need a spot of something pleasant today.* And that is all Moira needs to bring some pleasure to her morning.

After the morning meal is over, the tables cleared, dishes tucked into the dishwasher, and the floor swept, Moira hangs her apron on the back of the kitchen door and creeps quietly into her room for two aspirin and a lie-down before her housekeeping chores. She notices that Ioana has had the same idea for the ironing room door is shut tight and faint snores issue through the keyhole.

Moira awakes at mid-morning, revived and anxious to escape the confines of her small room. The writing group is laughing in the parlor as she passes by with the vacuum cleaner. What must it be like to write stories for others to read?

After her chores, she nods at Harold as she leaves the hotel. He is speaking on the telephone and tosses her a wink. Elated at his attention, she marches up the block toward the James Joyce Center, thinking to stop at the Cobalt Café across the street and have a fresh scone.

As she nears, she sees one of the Charles Stewart patrons studying the exhibition poster by the Center's doorway. It is the American lady with the frigid eyes, the one who looks like a ship about to leave harbor. Moira notes that the woman's cheeks are flushed as her eyes devour the picture of James Joyce.

A weedy looking man, Moira thinks. That lady, what is her name? Spelt, like the wheat; that's what Harold said. He knows so much and is always trying to improve Moira's mind. But this Spelt woman, she is flushed up like she is in love … over a picture? Fancy that. Blushing over some dead poet most people can't understand anyway.

She watches as Ms. Spelt drops her eyes to the sidewalk and gives a little gasp, all dramatic, fingers to open lips. What is it? Oh, dear heavens, she is picking up a dirty pigeon feather.

"Oh, you mustn't." Moira rushes to the woman's side. "They are full of germs; you might catch the bird flu or something."

Hannah Spelt raises her eyes, now filled with warmth as she grasps the feather to her chest, and then carefully tucks it into her purse without ruffling its vane. "It's a sign from him. After all this waiting."

"A sign? Like an omen, you mean?" Moira watches in bewilderment as the feather disappears into the woman's purse.

"Exactly." Hannah's face brightens at the girl who serves her two poached eggs, ham, and grilled tomatoes each morning. "Have you read James Joyce?"

"Only a bit in school." Moira is embarrassed by her lack of interest in the nation's greatest writer. "He's hard to understand."

"Of course, he is, my dear. He's trying to be as difficult as possible." Hannah glances over at the Cobalt Café and catches hold of Moira's elbow. "Come have a scone with me, and I'll explain him to you."

Filled with hot tea, a cinnamon scone, and more details on James Joyce than she will ever need, Moira waves goodbye as Hannah Spelt sails over to the Garden of Remembrance, still seeking her lost love. Moira heads down O'Connell Street toward the park with the Floozy in the Jacuzzi. Hannah Spelt said that the sculpture of woman reclining on a slope with water running about her is named Anna Livia and is a symbol of the River Liffey. Also, Anna Livia is one of her love James Joyce's characters who also represents the river, and wasn't that clever?

Moira doesn't know whether it is or not, but the bright sun pinks her skin as she walks. At the Liffy, she turns right on the quay, enjoying the light glistening on the river which, again according to Hannah, is the lifeblood of the city. Passing a coffee stand, she notices Cindy Turner, Room 101 at the Charles Stewart, a tall school teacher from Georgia who drawls all her words. The woman is absorbed in a book, so Moira scurries past. She has talked, or rather listened, enough for one afternoon.

And there is Anna Livia, still beautiful, having been removed from O'Connell Street over 10 years past and only uncrated and floated down the river to her new home a year ago. Moira remembers watching the barge float by and the cheers rising from the bystanders as Anna Livia passes by. Now that was history, not something by a dry, dead writer.

A sigh creeps past her lips. Another guest from the Charles Stewart. They seem to be littered all over Dublin today. It is the "Heavenly Warrior" man from Room 403. Oh my, he has removed his shirt and is lying on a concrete bench for the entire world to view.

Suddenly his eyes open with a dreamy gaze and he pushes himself up on his elbows. "Alana? Is that you?"

Moira looks all around, but she is the only one in evidence. Then he brushes the sleep from his eyes and frowns, the frown turns sad, and he looks thoroughly depressed.

"I didn't mean to disturb you, Mr. Shultz." Moira apologizes although she is guilty of nothing and makes a move to pass him.

"It's all right. I thought … well, I guess I was just dreaming. It's hard waiting for your true love to appear, you know that?" He looks at Moira as if she, despite her youth, might understand. He runs long fingers through his wavy hair which is tangled from the concrete.

"Yes, sir. Of course it is." She remembers waiting for Harold to notice her. Why it took all of four months, it seems, before he saw her as a real person. "Does she know you're here? In this park, I mean?"

He drops his eyes and studies his well-defined abdomen. "It doesn't seem so. At least not today."

Moira feels sorry for the man who is obviously waiting for someone he loves and who must not love him in return if she is making him wait like this.

"But perhaps tomorrow? And maybe on St. Stephen's Green. Lots of people go there."

He blinks, then rises, suddenly spurred to action. "Of course, a large park for all to see how special our love is. Tomorrow it is."

To Moira's horror, he begins to walk along beside her, forgetting that he is naked from neck to navel. Oh, how horrified her Granny would be at this. But then they pass a worker who had stripped off his shirt and is sunning his paper-white plump chest as he strides down the sidewalk. Moira appreciates how handsome and tan her companion is, gleaming hair flowing down his back, oblivious to everyone. She can never take him home to Howth though.

Alan Shultz bids her goodbye at the Heuston Station, thank heavens. Moira trudges back to the Charles Stewart, after picking up a pastie at a corner grocery. Time for tea and maybe she will read the brochure on James Joyce that Hannah Spelt has pressed on her.

With surprise she realizes she hasn't thought of Harold all afternoon, or of the blonde headed girl he was chatting up at the Temple Bar. Moira wondered why the girl was so upset with him. It is hard to imagine Harold mooning over anyone like Ms. Spelt or full of longing like the Heavenly Warrior, or even her for that matter.

Harold can't care less about toast the next morning. His complexion is the color of a china teacup; the roses of his cheeks have blanched away, the heavenly blue eyes washed almost clear as he sits silent before the Garda. His head never turns toward the front door.

Two large Garda fill the minute lobby and a trembling transit worker hangs on to the front desk. A murmuring crowd has gathered in the street outside, shooed back like so many chickens from the doorstep of the Charles Stewart by two more Garda.

Moira glances out the open front door and freezes, Harold's tea sloshing into the saucer, dampening the fresh-made toast. Is that an angel fallen from heaven on the steps, all gold and blue, like Mother Mary in her good robes? She looks down into the teacup to steady herself, wondering if there is an answer in the tea leaves.

"Ghastly." Harold murmurs the word with a cold clarity. "Like she was sleeping. I just opened the door when he knocked." *Him* is the gray-headed, gray-faced transit worker who keeps wringing large wrinkled hands. "He was pounding like mad and I didn't want him waking people."

Moira nods, her stomach trembling like his voice. "I've spoiled this. I'll fetch more. Running back down the hall, down the steps to the kitchen, she pours a new cup of tea. She added four spoons of sugar because that is what her Granny does in an emergency.

Today has taken on a fragile air, as if all need to be careful of how they place their feet, how deeply they breathe, how loudly they speak. If angels can fall to the steps of the Charles Steward, bruised and blue, then anything can happen to anyone.

Moira runs to tell Ioana, but Ioana has shut the door to the ironing closet and is nowhere to be found. In the end, it is the teacher, Cindy Turner, in Room 101 that she tells. And it is Cindy who gives her a reassuring hug before she dashes down the hall to the lobby, eager for this new turn of events in her life.

Moira goes back to her tiny bedroom in the basement and collapses on the cold hard mattress. She closes her eyes, trying to erase the vision on the front doorstep. Why did she keep thinking of Harold's blonde friend in the blue sweater, the one who walked away with despair on her face that night in the Temple Bar?

In a few minutes, voices begin to drift down through the vent in her ceiling and she sighs. There is only one spot in the upstairs hall where that can happen, and now people are standing there talking. She hears the buzz cut man, Mr. Moore, begin to pontificate on youth and the state of the world today. She can hear chirpy questions from Posey Mulvane, as if this terrible affair has suddenly lightened her mood. There is speculation the dead girl is pregnant and has killed herself. Little gasps come from the young Bridget, and Moira wonders if she agrees with everything Mr. Moore is saying, or is just too scared to go off by herself.

The day has been exhausting, worrying about Harold when he doesn't seem to care if she is nearby, listening to the strange inhabitants of the Charles Stewart revisit the dead girl over and over. Her eyes drowse shut.

When Moira awakes, the fallen angel in blue robes, blue bruises on her arms folded across her chest, sits in the single armchair. Her robes contrast nicely with the coral upholstery.

"You … you can't be here. You're dead." Moira pinches her wrist, but feels nothing.

"Death is only a bird feather falling to the ground. Death is waiting in the park for love that never comes. Death is broiled tomatoes and beans every morning."

"You're Harold's friend? From the Temple Bar?" Moira is astounded that her words come out in such a calm and steady fashion. "Why were you so upset with him?"

The angel bends her head, a sheath of blonde hair forming wings about her face. "Ah, what is a friend? What is love? Who can one believe?"

There is a banging on the door and Moira jolts awake with a gasp. Ioana is yelling through the keyhole.

"Now, Moira, come! The Garda are here again. More questions."

Moira doesn't want to leave the hard slab of her bed, the firm pillows. There is no comfort beyond the door.

At breakfast this morning the scent of beans brought back the tang of salt from the sea at Howth, the layered smells of fish, oysters, mussels, raw from the boats, processed in the factory, grilled, baked, fried at Ivan's, Beshoff's, and the Screaming Stream.

Dublin's sea scented air is mingled with exhaust from huge buses and many cars. Life is a constant thrum in the city. Moira feels she has expanded into someone worldlier, someone who has seen the Joyce Center and the Book of Kells, has heard all the local musicians in the pubs. But Dublin also holds broken angels on doorsteps and a plate of beans can still reduce her to tears.

Hannah in Dublin

MaryAnn L. Miller

There was just enough space between the handkerchief sized sink and the glass shelf above it for Hannah Spelt to fit her face as she brushed her teeth. She would not be able to take a birdbath in this sink. One of her boobs would not even fit into it. She cracked her head on the shelf as she startled at the slam against the one tall window. It was a dark feathered pigeon, now lying on its back murmuring, its pink feet in the air, its head pressed back against the mossy stone floor of the tiny courtyard. Hannah watched as the bird miraculously roused itself, flew up up out and over the roof of the Charles Stewart Guesthouse. She took this event as a sign. She had come to the right place on O'Connell Street here in the center of Dublin. James, the love of her life was near. Hannah named the pigeon Joyce and would later remember that day as "the day Joyce-hit-the-window."

That day Hannah began toying with the notion that perhaps she had been Irish in another life and perhaps she was the Galway Girl made famous in song, and regaled, she would discover, in every pub. Instead of a retired benefits administrator from Erie, Pennsylvania, she was the Galway Woman who went from pub to pub dancing, inviting her long lost poet to appear and dance with her. She felt young again, not in the pierced, painted hair way of the girls at the Charles Stewart like Posey and Bridget, but in the post-menopausal zest way that only an older woman can experience. Hannah looked herself in her icy blue eyes, surveyed the fit of her aqua cashmere sweater and sailed like an ocean liner out the door to sit for a while in the Garden of Remembrance across Parnell Square. She thought it might be a cemetery. Hannah wanted to conjure up ghosts and give herself chills as she planned her day.

Hannah had to halt her progress to avoid the hubbub on the front steps. Someone had died on the stone stairs of the Charles

Stewart during the early morning hours. Red lights were flashing. The EMTs were picking up the limp body of a platinum-haired girl, zipping her into a black plastic body bag. The poor thing was staring at the sky with a stunned face. Hannah thought she saw a dark feather drift from the bag. She picked it up having an urge to return it, but the girl was being loaded into the ambulance. She tucked it into her small leather purse. Hannah crossed the street and then suddenly ran back again shouting to the medics,

"What's her name? Is her name Joyce?"

They closed the doors.

"We don't know what she's called," one of them said.

As Hannah sat on one of the wooden benches in the Garden of Remembrance, a pigeon swooped over her and landed on the stone path. It strutted on its delicate coral feet pecking at stone dust. Hannah pulled the feather from her purse.

"Oh! It matches! Joyce, thank God you're okay. Don't ever leave me!"

This line of thinking did not necessarily make sense but Hannah did not care. She would never have picked up a pigeon feather at home. Everyone said they were vermin. She knew, in the end, Joyce would fly away, but for now she was comforted believing the bird was her guide and would stay forever. Eventually, everyone always left. Hannah couldn't abide anyone else leaving so she had left herself. She had left her old self behind. Sitting in the Garden of Remembrance under the sculpture of human figures turning into upward flying swans made her certain that she would change into the woman she was meant to be. It also unleashed a stream of memory, a flow of loss, through her mind: her father hit in the head by a drifting boxcar as he bent to oil the coupling. He would have loved the trains here in Dublin even though a train had been the death of him. Hannah could hear his voice ring out from his recliner as she made supper each evening while he worked the daily crossword.

"How do you spell corpse?"

She would answer and he always thanked her in his countrified way, "Thankee, Hannah."

He had been born in the wilds of Western Pennsylvania in 1938 to parents who had come from West Virginia. His speech was a kind of poetry all to itself. Hannah missed most his storytelling. He would take off his rimless glasses and blink back tears as he recited tales from childhood and his years with the railroad that he insisted on calling the Erie & Lackawanna, although it hadn't been that since 1960.

There was the story of the white horse that he and his brothers had thought was a ghost as it raised its head above the neighbor's hedge. They ran in silent terror from their night of orchard raiding. There was the story of a woman who ran off with an Indian. Her family caught them, tied him to a tree and started to burn him when the sheriff stopped them, just as the Indian's pant leg caught fire. None of Hannah's men friends had such interesting things to talk about. Daddy Spelt would be proud that Hannah had set out on her own to find her true life. Of course, she'd been set free sooner than she'd ever dreamed of because of that drifting boxcar. She owed her early retirement to that fatal bonk on the head. Conrail had settled over a million dollars onto Hannah and she had the proceeds from the sale of Daddy Spelt's house.

"This place is already staged!" the realtor had exclaimed.

Hannah with her decorator friend Patty Cooney had redone the house at least three times over the years. It was Patty Cooney's trip to Ireland five years ago that got Hannah thinking about James and her long ago crush on him.

"What are you going to do with yourself now that you're a lady of leisure?"

Hannah knew exactly the answer to that question. When she gave her notice she had already formed the vision that lodged in her heart since high school. She would travel to Ireland and find a grand passion. She couldn't tell anyone, even Patty Cooney, because Hannah thought it would sound juvenile. Besides, what if she failed. No one needed to know how childish she could be. She would say yes to everything, although she had already nixed the Tuesday afternoon mahjong club of retirees in her apartment complex.

Hannah's credo, she realized, was "Now or never" and "What if?" What if she flew to Dublin? What if she relied only on herself? What if she wiped out the dreary routines of others that she had followed for years? She had no one to answer to but herself. There was someone out there waiting for her. He would be her exact match—mysterious, hard to know, intellectual—her high school literary hero James Joyce. Her resolve strengthened as she gazed at the only photo of James that she had ever seen. His Irish eyes like the sea, his bony face, and the erotic set of his lovely round glasses. Once he set those penetrating eyes on Hannah, she knew he would return the passion that she felt. Words would pour out of him in a romantic shower of beautiful lilting language. She squirmed beneath the vague gaze of the photo. A fleeting vision of the dead girl of that morning passed her inner eye. Now or never. It had to be now.

Hannah had been at the Charles Stewart for three days and still couldn't bring herself to approach any of the other guests. They were always in the hall outside her room and every time she left her room she heard footsteps around the corner but when she turned the corner, no one was ever there. They must be ducking into their rooms too quickly for her to meet them in the narrow, carpeted hallway. She knew they were going out to pubs at night and longed to go along but didn't want to have to talk to them. On the day of the dead girl, yesterday, she had seen three or four of the young women chattering with the neatly dressed man in #109. As she got her morning tea and oatcakes in the breakfast room, Hannah heard the girls at the back table twittering, "Here's James!"

She snapped to attention and turned to see whom they were talking about. It was the neatly dressed man who looked like an insurance salesman with a stick up his ass. It pleased Hannah to think so freely—she never would have allowed herself to even think the word "ass." Now she's like to say it aloud- soon. Also "feck." First chance she got that would come out of her mouth. This James was obviously not the one she wanted—too young, too American, and too unpoetic. He flirted tentatively with the girls, especially the teacher who kept talking about her tiny students and their need for her.

The one person Hannah felt halfway comfortable with was Ioana who approached her with a smile each morning. Hannah towered over her. Ioana's eyes were level with Hannah's bosom. When Ioana came toward her, Hannah immediately sat down to avoid the embarrassing proximity.

"My name is your name in Rumanian: Hannah--Ioana, same thing. What part of Ireland are you from?"

Hannah knew an opportunity when she saw it. "Galway," she said. Gesturing for Ioana to come closer, she whispered in her ear in her best Irish accent. "That James, he has a fecking stick up his ass. Yeah?"

Ioana's eyes opened in surprise. She smacked her hand on the table and laughed.

"Yeah!" she said. Hannah had her pipeline to the pubs.

She made a date with Ioana for 9:30 that same night to walk to The Celt not far from the Millennium Needle about five blocks down O'Connell Street. But now, she was headed for the Irish Writer's Centre just up the street from the Charles Stewart. There she would start her hunt for the real James.

The orders painted on the street annoyed Hannah. She wanted to Look Right when she should Look Left. Yesterday, a Sunday, she simply ran across in front of the Guesthouse, no traffic to interfere. Today, buses were slamming by and cars were turning from nowhere. She couldn't think and was almost run down by a woman on a bicycle just when she thought she was safely across.

"Hey!" shouted the helmeted young woman.

Hannah glared at her and continued on. *Brazen bitch,* she thought as she climbed the stone stairs into the Writers' Museum, mistaking it for the Writers' Centre. The man at the desk rose and came around to greet her.

"How can I find James Joyce?" Hannah asked?

"Oh, just walk right across the street and take your second right. His house is about halfway down on the left side, or you can just go in there," he gestured to a closed white door. "Your choice."

"How long a walk is it?'

"Oh, a good two hours," he said. Hannah's full lips drooped.

"I'm joking!" he said. "It's only five minutes. Puzzled, Hanna said she'd go to the Joyce house first then come back to the Centre.

"Oh, this isn't the Centre, it's the Museum. The Centre is a couple of doors down."

Could she believe him? She looked around. She was indeed in the Museum, a simple mistake. It didn't matter.

The odor of bus exhaust met her on the street. Her thin-soled flats caused Hannah to pick her way gingerly along the cobbled street. She passed the Cobalt Café on the right and spotted the Joyce house on the other side of the street. She was chagrined to find James' house open to the public with people streaming in and out, and she had to buy a ticket to enter. Probably his rooms were private. She asked the girl at the desk, "Where would James' rooms be?"

"His room is on the third floor. Go all the way up." At the top of the house, she encountered two doors each labeled "Enter." She chose the left half thinking a bus might come at her. It opened into a small foyer and she was directly in James' bedroom. What a mess. Clothes strewn around, books and other personal items, and it looked like a woman also lived here. How one person could fit into that tiny space let alone two, Hannah didn't know. It looked like Harry Potter's nest under the stairs. James definitely needed her, and he could use Patty Cooney, too. Hannah could contribute her love and resources. Surely more of the house could be redecorated. Otherwise, they would have to live somewhere else. Hannah could never live in this tiny space, and as for the woman; she was probably just a convenience. A virile man like James would, of course, not be celibate.

By the end of that day, Hannah dreams would be evaporated. She sat stunned in the adjacent room watching a video about James and his wife, Nora Barnacle, a fitting name for someone who could not be pried away. They were both dead. James had not even lived in Ireland since 1906. Hannah decided to experience the full catastrophe of her ignorance. She hurried back to the Museum, paid her entry fee and blushed at the clerk's jovial words.

"So did you find the house? Were you worn out looking for it?"

Hannah mumbled, "Yes, and I still am."

After Hannah wore herself out further reading all the installations about Irish writers and poets in the Museum, she went into the café for a salad and a scone and a cup of tea. There was newness in her heart, an emptiness. She felt foolish and saw herself as naïve. She would never allow herself to be so stupid again. She needed some education and she needed to talk herself out of this ridiculous obsession. Hannah gathered herself for a visit to the Irish Writer's Centre.

There Hannah became a member of the Ink Slingers Creative Writing Workshop. It met every Saturday at 1:30. She considered the workshop a good use of her funds. She had ninety days before she'd have to leave the country. She was determined to be changed, but not in the crazy way she had thought.

There was no reason why she couldn't still love James' writing, the little she had read of it, but there were so many other writers to learn about. If she tried to write poetry herself, she would gain even more of an appreciation. Her thoughts constantly flew forward to Saturday and her first session with the Ink Slingers. In the meantime, Hannah went online at the Charles Stewart to find herself some dancing lessons. She was getting herself some new obsessions. She kept trying to miss the old one, but just couldn't summon up that useless passion.

Dance lessons were held upstairs at the Glenside Pub on Tuesday nights and the new term was starting the first week of April, a mere seven days away. Women on their own were welcome, and it was only ten euros a session. All you had to do was show up for two hours of dance lessons.

That night with Ioana, Hannah observed the drunks dancing at The Celt. They would caper about like goats or stagger dance around the tiny space in front of the band, but there were a few people who seemed to be doing formal steps and responding to each other's moves. When these people danced the other drinkers applauded and whistled. There was some standard of excellence that went on that was being recognized.

"The *craic* is good tonight, yeah?" Ioana yelled in her ear.

Hannah nodded in agreement, not wanting to sound ignorant by asking what that was. She watched closely as a woman got up to dance alone to Galway Girl. This woman was built like

Hannah with thin legs and small feet and a monumental bosom that jiggled slightly as she traced circles on the floor with her shoes. Each step was an invitation, and soon a saggy-faced bald man jostled his way around Hannah to answer the call. They danced facing one another with their hands clasped behind their backs. The woman's upper back was stooped. Hannah remembered her mother's admonishment, "Always keep your back straight and your chin up. Carry yourself with pride. You are a woman now and can never be mistaken for a girl." Hannah was fourteen and wanted to hide her massive presence. Those words would support Hannah all through the agony of losing her mother two years after that to breast cancer, her best asset becoming the death of her. Hannah couldn't know then, and she was not to know for years, that she, too, carried the mutation that would turn her into her mother.

Her time in Dublin was almost over. Hannah had spent her days learning how to write poetry and her evenings taking dance lessons or having fun in the pubs. She loved the Celt and O'Shea's down the street. The first time she dared dance, the saggy-faced bald man leapt up to join her. The rhythmic clapping swelled and Hannah never had to buy her own drinks again. The last week of her Dublin sojourn she invited her new friends and the current guests at the Charles Stewart to hear her read her best poem at the Ink Slingers final reading of the season. As she waited her turn to read on that balmy summer evening, Hannah noted the pigeons in the Garden of Remembrance across the square. The day Joyce hit the window seemed years behind her. Hannah had found her poet, and it was herself.

Galway Woman by Hannah Spelt

The Galway woman dances

    water over sand

        moving pebbles with her soft shoes.

Hands behind her she dreams

of someone she might

want to touch.

Throw his round glasses to the floor

crush his hat

into the boards.

He would loosen his grip on the pen

give his feet to the dance

his ears to the yelps and

whistles of admirers

beating the rhythm out of him.

The fiddle ends, the Galway woman

and tonight's James, their

bodies not quite touching,

    glide to a table in the dark

        sip the bitter rich foam

           near the banks of the Liffey.

Heavenly Warrior

Tracy Robert

Ireland reminds him, for some inexplicable reason, of his ancient French grandmother—the one from whom he hoped he'd inherited longevity genes—overdressing for the summer opera in casual Laguna Beach. The old woman did herself up as if she were still a resident of Paris: black silk sheath, topped by a sweater that scared him as a boy because a dead, skinned fox—head and all—formed its collar. She wore three-inch heels and clambered up the brick steps to the outdoor amphitheatre. She walked in those heels with the tentative enjoyment of little girls playing dress-up games, scuffing and prancing unsteadily. "Are you sure you want to wear those, Grandma?" he said.

"Of course I am," she replied, and took his arm firmly, in the same way thoughts of Ireland had seized him and not released. She's been gone twenty years, but never let go of her high heels. She was buried in them.

Buried, Alan thinks, like those love-and-dread-filled years he lived as Destiny did her ultimate best to survive chronic lymphocytic leukemia. Doctors had said—not promised, but said— that with treatment and appropriate dietary and lifestyle adjustments her condition was manageable, and for some years that had been true. Both of them ate organic and worked out daily until her white count dropped to zero and she caught a cold. Within a week, Destiny was gone, her green tea eyes veiled by the distance between breath and no breath. No one believed Destiny was her actual given name, from birth till the day she died. So what did it matter that he changed his lackluster name to Heavenly Warrior when he resigned his position as CPA at Prudential Financial to become a Spiritual and Physical Life Coach? Not everyone had the coping skills necessary for life on complex Planet Earth. He left his cosmos-blue postcards under windshield wipers, and gained a following. It appeared that his services were needed because business had grown to the degree that he required a partner, but not just any partner. A helpmate. A soulmate to help him love again.

So here he is in Dublin, stubborn grand dame of a city, where people keep the indoor heat cranked up even when it is a balmy 22 degrees Celsius outside. As he meditates, gulping in air by his room's tiny window, he thinks of that edifice of an American woman, Hannah, daintily wiping sweat from her face with a greasy napkin in the breakfast room of the Charles Stewart.

The helpmate first came to him months before in a vision brought on by a week-long liquid fast of wheat grass and Goji berry juice: his soulmate, Alana to his Alan. He was weary of being the lone Heavenly Warrior, teaching people how to feed and build their sadly neglected bodies. Alana would help him. She would be as committed to sculpting her structure as he was and they would maintain superior body health until the cure for aging was found and they became Alan and Alana unto eternity. His vision had placed her on the James Joyce Bridge, that lean, graceful architectural expanse over the River Liffey. He's camped by the river two days and one evening straight now but Alana hasn't appeared. The only women he's come to recognize are the pierced and tattooed waif down the hall who looks like a hairdryer would blow her out the window, a piece of dandelion fluff, and Hannah, immovable as a piano. Even her skinny legs look piano-like, supporting that voluminous torso.

He seeks a woman of skin, bone, and, yes, muscle. Alana, who eludes him.

His window is thrown wide open and has been since his arrival. The weather holds, unseasonably warm, and all the heat of the building rises to his floor, the 4th and final. After completing five sets of turbo crunches, his pores weep sweat, the navy floral carpet blackening beneath him. Now he'll have to wedge his broad shoulders into the pneumatic tube of a shower to prepare for late afternoon bridge watch.

Three mornings later, hearing more than the usual bus stop hubbub, Alan thrusts his entire torso out the open window to glimpse the source of excitement. It is then he sees the body of a young woman moved from the hotel's steps to the sidewalk, then covered gingerly with a blanket that couldn't possibly warm her. This is no one he's seen at the Charles Stewart or on his Alana watch at the river. This is a pale stranger who has given up on caring for her earthly body.

The breakfast room murmurs with fascinated gossip about the corpse; the words *runaway* and *overdose* and *notification of kin* pepper the intensified air. Alan requests three poached eggs and no bacon rashers, thank you. No toast. What if the corpse were his Alana? Nonsense. She simply can't be. His Alana wouldn't permit herself to die in resignation. But the angelic vision of the blue-dressed girl haunts him throughout the day's vigil at the James Joyce Bridge. And for the first time since his original vision and the execution of his plan to visit Dublin and claim his soulmate, he begins to doubt he'll recognize her if she appears to him.

Why in the name of everything achievable is he thinking this way? Hadn't he packed his crystals, heartbreak healing rose quartz included, along with his lucky seagull gray leather-bound Bible? The mission had initially been so clear to him: find a woman with gold hair that fell in cascades around her face, gliding in a gown-like dress—the color was sky blue—across the James Joyce Bridge in the brilliant March sunshine. The poor dead girl had been dressed in blue, which could be why he's caught in a lapse of faith. Well, the girl's gone. Nothing will erase that. He mentally recites a warrior's prayer for the departed in order to exorcise the cloud of negative energy the corpse's image surrounds him with, and repeats the prayer several times, ending with, "In the name of all that makes me what I am and growing stronger, amen."

He, Alan Shultz, Heavenly Warrior, will redouble his watch for Alana. Death, a part of the universal cycle, happens every day whether he sees it or not. He is too young to be doubting himself, and too old to waste time. Alana might reveal herself during the thirty minutes he breaks for lunch, so now he resolves to bring the meal, gathering what he can from the farmer's market off Henry Street.

At lunch, as Alan chews a pulpy, juiceless tangerine to mush, there's a scuffle on the bridge—a voice hollering what seems to be the word *joy* or maybe *joys,* a walloping swath of white tunic and metallic blue neck scarf—and Heavenly Warrior, before he can help himself, is hanging on to a trembling Hannah, keeping her feet on the ground as she leans precariously out over the River Liffey to catch a feather.

Ioana of the European Cultural Center

Andy Sachar

The first week of spring was unseasonably warm. No rain, no clouds, and by the end of the week no coats. It took a while to soak in. Dubliners exposed their fleshy white shoulders and their pink knees, and their Irish cheeks slowly reddened as the week marched forth.

Ioana says weather reports here are as disconnected as they were in Romania. Anyone on the streets of Dublin during that magical summer week in late March will tell you that the temperatures reported were 10 degrees lower than the way it really was.

"But," says Ioana, "I guess people just believe what they are told."

James, the neighbor from room 109, who had no idea he was her neighbor, today in a red checked shirt just like yesterday's blue checks, explained it to her when she brought his breakfast to his table. "Yes, I know it feels much warmer to you, but that's just an illusion. Science will tell you otherwise. Look. See. It was just 64 degrees yesterday."

Ioana stared at him and frowned.

James gave her a crooked smile and a slight shrug.

She placed the fried egg and ugly gelatinous sausages in front of him, not smiling.

Ioana pulls the red chair, the only chair, up to her bed, which will now cease being her bed and become her table. The bed and the chair were all the furniture that could squeeze into the room.

She pulls the Cornish pasty from the white paper bag, tears the bag into a flat sheet, and uses it as a plate. The pasty, still almost too hot to touch, cost 4.80 euro during the day at the Cesta market on the corner, but Ari, the East Indian man behind the cash register, sells her any of his leftover hot deli pastries for just 1 Euro before closing at 10 PM.

She bites into steaming potatoes and vegetables, flakey bits of puff pastry fluttering onto the flayed white bag.

Moira, just 19-years-old, caught her 4-inch purple heel in a sidewalk grate and would have probably landed flat on the concrete if she her arm hadn't already been hanging over Ioana's shoulder as they swayed down the street.

Which was good luck for Moira but quite enough for Ioana, who will to have to do neck stretches tonight if she expected to iron sheets again in the morning. Loud music and cheap vodka was not the rebellious escape it might have been should she still be Moira's age.

Still, reckless as Moira had been tonight, it was comforting to be two stumbling down the late night street, not just a her normally tight stepping self in unfamiliar territory where the Midnight Rambler might be licking his chops in the shadows.

And a relief to wobble through the darkness to end up in her tiny nest at the Charles Stewart. Unlike the always apprehensive climb up the stairs to her flat on Aleea Taberei 6377, Sector A, Floor 8, room 19 in Sibiu, where she might find Huratiu waiting, demanding to know where she had been and who she had met.

On Tuesday morning, Ioana found herself carrying eggs and bacon and sausage and beans to the guests at the Charles Stewart. And tomatoes.

"A fried egg and sausage," she mumbled to herself.

"A fried egg and sausage," said the man in the checkered shirt from 109, her next door neighbor this week, although he had no idea. Time stopped for a moment when she looked at him, really looked at him.

She wanted to say, "No, not the sausage. It's tasteless. Or, rather, okay, nothing is tasteless, but tasteless would be better. Why not try the thick and salty bacon this time? A tomato? And let me sprinkle a little pepper on your egg today."

She almost added, "And you might try wearing a different kind of shirt tomorrow." Instead, she said to him, "I'm going to do something today that I've been wanting to do."

Ioana cringed when Horatiu stepped toward her, but he didn't shove her or even scowl at her. He merely cupped has hands on her shoulders lightly, his big hands on the clean white cotton shoulders of her t-shirt, to show her that he cared for her and that he wasn't going to hurt her. And he wasn't going to let her back away, either.

Inscribed in blue and orange on her t-shirt: Sibiu–European Capital of Culture 2007. Ioana was proud of that t-shirt, proud of her city's status, and proud of her own small part in it.

Horatiu looked imploringly into her eyes. Which were hazel that day, at least in the soft light of her flat with its pale plaster walls. His own eyes were inky black. His round face, that day, red.

Ioana drew a sharp breath, mouth closed, and stared back at him, eyes clear and for once, not squinty.

"I told you I will not hit you again," said Horatiu. "and I will not hit you."

She breathed through her nose and said nothing, her muscles still tightening.

"Ioana," he said. "I can't hurt you. I love you." He smiled at her when he said this, like a father explaining to a child. She could smell the garlic on his breath. He asked quietly, "Do you love me?" And then he answered his own question. "I know you do."

She just stared at him, afraid to move, looking up into that round face, his dark wavy hair, those long black eyelashes that were once so appealing and now so appalling.

"Ioana, tell me that you love me."

"Hori, I told you I cannot be in this relationship anymore." She felt his hands tightened on her shoulders. "Please. You know I can't stay with someone I'm afraid of."

He scowled and shook her a bit, losing control of his frustration, but just a little bit.

"No," she said. "Don't hit me."

He slowly released his grip and backed away. "I can't hit you. I promised. I love you."

Maybe he wouldn't hurt her now. He seemed to be in control. But she knew that his anger would begin to grow when he left, and he could come back in wild fury. If he lets go of her shoulders and lets her out of his sight, then she really must leave. Now. Passport ready. Backpack packed. Good-bye to the Capital of Culture and the Theatre Thalia.

Ioana tried to keep her breathing steady.

"Look," said Horatiu. "You want to slow our relationship, too strong too fast, all that. Clear. But I need to hear that you love me."

"Hori...."

"You don't even have to mean it. I know that you're afraid. I just want to hear the words."

Ioana turned her head, deep brown hair momently hiding her face. "Hori, I can't do this..."

"Just humor me. Just say, 'Hori, I love you.' I need to hear that one more time."

"Hori?"

"Ioana, just one last time tell me you love me, and I will take that with me and leave."

"Hori, you can't force me to say this. You can't ask me this when you're holding me so I can't move! This scares me!"

Horatiu dropped his hands to his sides, and took a step back. "Okay. I understand," he said. But now, please, just tell me. You know me. One last time, and I leave in peace. Even if you don't feel it. Tell me you love me and you're very sorry you have to break up with me"

"I can't say that." Ioana is now getting a little angry. "I won't mean it. I'm afraid of you. "

"Just say it," said Horatiu. "One last request. It will make it easier for me."

Ioana took a deep breath, this time through her mouth.

"Okay, she said, and looked down at her tennis shoes. She looked back at Horatiu again, and said, as if on stage, "Hori, I love you. I'm sorry I have to leave, but I do have to leave."

Huratio stared at her. He folded his hands over his chest, biceps compressing. "Do you mean it?" he asked. "I mean, I know I asked you to say that, but did you feel anything when you said it? I think you did."

"I feel sorry about everything, but that's all. Just sorry."

He moved in and grabbed her shoulders again. "You don't love me?"

She looked straight into his inky black eyes, her own eyes now mostly brown. "Hori, I do not love you."

He shoved her, and she smashed hard against the wall.

"Curvă!" he sneered.

He thundered out of her flat, slamming the door and banging his way down the hallway.

Dublin stays up late and wakes up early. Ioana had expected a hidden fog of a city that would gradually piece by piece make itself clear. Instead, it was like Sibiu, a tourist town, a place where people came to roam the streets for the cafes and the music and the theaters.

But Ioana wasn't a street musician. And somehow the restaurants didn't buy her lie about waiting tables in Romania. And she wasn't Irish.

The city was too big to just walk in and announce oneself. And too small not to. Too many others interested in theater, probably already connected, their English impeccable. Is there someone out there looking for a skinny Romanian actor with a strong accent?

So she smoothed an endless pile of sheets with her hot iron in a tiny workroom in the Charles Stewart. Too foreign to be a accepted, they saw only what they expected.

It was mid-March, and the days were longer and the rain was softer and Ioana decided it was time to come out into the sunshine.

Ioana is clearly excited. "You just stand up straight and speak with authority and they will accept what you say!

"Something happened?"

"I might be an intern."

Hannah surprised herself with a shriek of delight, suddenly she is Ioana's age. "Ioana!"

She studies the skinny girl with those squinty eyes and perpetual energy.

"And you really can do Photoshop?"

"And Dreamweaver," says Ioana pulling on her stringy hair. "Moira's idea. I told her how all computer programs are free in Romania."

"Free?"

"Sort of free," says Ioana.

Hannah frowns theatrically, "So no more Charles Stewart."

"Oh no, no. I will stay. I can sleep there at the Charles Stewart. I get paid there. The marketing agency is more like going to school.

They are sitting in the garden at the Cobalt Cafe, with shiny smoked salmon and fresh bread and the most delicate salad dressing that Ioana has ever encountered.

"Hannah, thank you so much. I will take you out for a meal some day soon."

Hannah smiles at her, her hair piled high to keep her neck cool. "You already bring me extra bacon every morning."

"You know what I mean."

And then Ioana's usually scrunched eyes widen, turns out they are hazel again today, and she shudders visibly. She shakes her head and stares forward, jolted, terrified.

Hannah looks up intently. "What just happened?"

Ioana takes in a quick breath, then she brings her hands to her face, tears spilling over her cheeks. "I don't know," Ioana said. "I don't know!

Hannah places her hand on Ioana's wiry arm. "Horatiu?" she asks quietly. "Is it Horatiu again?"

Ioana sobs. "Yes. Horatiu. Something is going to happen. Something is happening."

Hannah waits a long minute and speaks softly to her new young friend. "Nothing will happen. Ioana. He can't hurt you anymore. Ever. He's far away. You left him. He's gone."

"It's my fault. I know he wants to find me. Do you think I should return?"

Hannah tightens her grip on Ioana's arm. "Ioana, he's gone."

Ioana, exhales deeply and allows a sheepish smile to break through.

Hannah doesn't let go.

Then with a sharp mew, the call of the city, a large pigeon alights on their table, it's wings beating like the urgent crossing alert of the Dublin traffic lights: takka takka takka takka takka takka takka takka.

"Oh my God, It's Joyce!" cries Hannah. "Look! See, Ioana? My relationship is so much better now. Everything's fine!"

Ioana laughs and slowly stretches out her finger to caress the bird, delighted that it doesn't fly away.

Joe O'Brien, the first garda on the scene at Parnell and O'Connell stepped back over the yellow police tape as the ambulance zoomed away, blue lights afire, and again he opened the passport, remarkably clean of blood and dirt. Second death this week on O'Connell Street.

"Smacked by a two decker turning off O'Connell," remarked Fitzpatrick, flatly.

O'Brien shook his head gravely. "Romanian passport. Even if he saw the LOOK RIGHT painted on the curb, this guy maybe didn't have enough English to even get it." He leafed through the passport.

Annie Donnelly, one of the onlookers, repeated what she'd already told O'Brien. She stepped back and forth and moved her hands when she talked. Donnelly was a slightly pudgy young woman, low cut t-shirt exhibiting a bushel of powder white skin bobbling in the unseasonal sunshine.

She bobbled and babbled, "So he stepped out across the street, and he made it to the median, but I guess, I mean he didn't realize, he didn't look, and he walked out, and the bus turned, and he froze. Right there. He froze there. But he turned, he turned like to jump back to the median, but then right then, exactly in that split second, the bus turning and the bird came, and it flew right in his face, I mean right in his face, and the bus was coming, and I think the bird must have been as shocked as the guy because it sort of shrieked, and well, you know.   It was terrible.   It was really terrible. SMACK!!!" I mean SMACK!! And SMUSCHH!"

"Flattened like a rasher of bacon," agreed Fitzpatrick.

The Way Out

Jeanne Goldberg-Leopold

Bridget got up to fill the tiny cup with more watery coffee, trying not to admit that she missed the strong Chemex drip she had at home. Moira, the plump sweet kitchen help who reminded her of her friend Kathy, came up to her and whispered, "Did you hear about the girl they found on the step this morning?"

"No- what......?"

"Dead as a doornail. Found her beaten up, looking up to heaven. Tiny blonde thing she was, kind of like you."

"What happened to her? Who did it?" Bridget asked.

"Don't know," Moira said and hurried off to bring runny eggs and beans to the muscle man who was down the hall from her. He would sprinkle them with seeds and green flakes from the plastic bag in his pocket.

Bridget sat down with her coffee, wishing Nadia hadn't slept in, so that she would have someone to talk to. "*That* could have been me." She thought. If she had gotten that job at the Blissful Massage and Manicure Salon across from The Celt, she might have met a guy coming out of the tattoo parlor next door; a guy with a fresh, aching tattoo of a serpent coiling around his biceps. They could have sat down by the river drinking cheap beer and then who knows what would have happened.

That could have been me," she said softly out loud and a chill went through her. Suddenly the big city seemed a little scary, reminding her of the creepy sculptures in her living room at home. Still, the thought of the quiet streets of Killiney, the soothing lap of the bay water, the fresh feel of the sea air, the comfort of knowing almost everyone she would meet, made her want to cry.

Hearing about the dead girl found on the steps made something snap inside Bridget. It was like the time she went to take the history test on the early Chinese empires. She had studied and was so confident until the test was placed in front of her. Then, it was like reading a foreign language- like being lost in a forest and not knowing the way out.

Sitting on the hard bed with its scratchy blue brocade bedspread, Bridget can barely admit to herself that she wishes she was sitting on her lavender flowered duvet covered bed at home, picked out by her mother for the girl she wished Bridget would be. Most of all, she longs to hold her Pandy bear, now black and grey, instead of black and white; one eye glaucoma-ed from age and being dragged against the floor; one ear bitten by Bootsy when he was a puppy.

She rubs her eyes, her right hand bumping into her nose ring and reminding her she is too old for this. She has come to the big city to escape the dull sameness of Killiney. The endless hours of nothing to do but look at the rain falling and the grass getting greener and greener. The same people, averted glances, hands over mouths, whispering, gossiping, and judging. She can see her mother, lips moving constantly, spewing words of negativity, "No, no. Don't do that. You shouldn't. You can't. Damn you." Her stepfather -- what right did he have -- echoing her mother. "I have a good mind to take you over my knee…"

"Oh yeah, just try it", she says. "You're not my father".

Her father, her father. She is in her footed yellow pj's, sitting on his lap. She smells the stale cigarette smokiness of him and the peppermint candy to mask it. He opens the book with a crackle and pulls her close to him. She had just started at St. Francis when he died. Six long years there, without him. She closes her eyes and can't conjure up his face, but memories of school day haunt her.

Soon as she crosses Wood Street and nears the steps of St. Francis, Bridget realizes she has forgotten to roll down her skirt. She juggles her book satchel and with one hand unrolls the four inches of plaid caught up in her waistband. There,- that avoids one demerit. Check. Her hands flit to her ear and she deftly removes one large hoop earring and then another. Check- another demerit avoided. She spits out her gum into an old math test. Check- three demerits prevented before the first bell. It is going to be a good day. Well, as good as it can be sitting in school listening to fecking idiots drone on about nothing. If she could make it through Theology second period then she might be able to survive until lunch.

But making it through Theology is easier said than done. Ms. Kady marches into the classroom, her soft pink cardigan impeccably matched to the flowered long sleeved blouse and coordinated with the delicate pink pearl stud earring and matching necklace. Ms. K, a young woman with an old woman's moral views, likes precision. Bridget does not, and these forty-five minutes are a daily challenge.

After the prayer asking God to forgive them for all their sins, Ms. Kady announces that the lesson for the day is on chastity, the greatest gift a girl can give to Jesus. "OMG," Bridget texts quickly to Megan, under the cover of the desk. "Hasn't Jesus gotten enough gifts already? Why not give to the poor?"

"Young ladies," Ms. Kady goes on. "It is your Christian duty to save yourself for marriage. It is what our Lord, Jesus Christ wants --expects -- you to do."

Too dangerous to text now as Ms. Kady is walking around the room, striking desks with her hand, emphasizing her point, looking into the eyes of girls she believes are doomed. She does not look at Bridget, but she should have. Bridget knows what she would have texted to Megan if she could. "This witch doesn't know what the feck she's talking about. How could she even know what she's missing?"

Bridget shakes her head and rubs her eyes, trying to dispel the memory. She has left that all behind. She tries to focus on her new life here in Dublin. She can hardly believe that Moira is only two years older. She grew up in a little dull town, too, and settled in the big city, found a job and is living on her own. She seems so sure of herself, so confident, and happy with her soft curved body. "Oh, where is my mind going?" Bridget stops herself. She would have to talk more to Moira, find out how she did it. Maybe if I can get a job at the Blissful Massage and Nail Parlor or somewhere, we could become friends, go out for a pint. Someone to talk to besides Nadia who is never around.

Bridget pushes the resistant door closed and throws the heavy key ring onto the table. The ping of metal and wood breaking the silence. The room has been cleaned and everything is neat and orderly. She takes in the simplicity, the tightly made blue brocade bedspread and matching curtains, like something her grandmother would have. Except that her grandmother would clutter the room with junk: kissing leprechauns, shamrocks with smiley faces, and porcelain figurines of Mary cradling Baby Jesus. But none of that here. Just a plain wooden table and two old-fashioned chairs, a large wooden closet, ugly night stands, and a tiny TV, which served no purpose as it only got three channels. Why her laptop had a bigger screen and she could watch almost anything she wanted.

Still, it is a relief to be here, away from the carefully decorated home of her mother and stepfather. No weird monster-like modern sculptures greeting you, no need to worry about not putting a designer pillow exactly back in its place. And most important, there was quiet -- no squabbling little brother, no one screaming at her to do this or that or telling her that she was a total feck-up. She doesn't need anyone to tell her that.. She's glad Nadia isn't here now.

How lucky she is that Nadia invited her to come to the Charles Stewart after she finished being an au pair for her brothers. Even if the dead girl on the steps frightened her, going back home is scarier. Maybe it is time to leave the Charles Stewart and the ghost of the dead girl. Time to move on to another, better life. She can picture herself as a tour guide at the Guinness Factory, earning enough money to share a flat with a girl like Moira. She takes out her nose ring and gets ready for a trip to the pharmacy to get hair-dye to make her hair all red. First steps on her way to a new, independent life.

■■

Replaced

Nancy W. Shumaker

Cindy Turner finished her full Irish breakfast, pushed the white crockery plate to one side, and sat back to check out the other occupants of the dining room. She liked the variety of people at the Charles Stewart. The Gresham down the street was a classier hotel but it looked boring, full of stuffy, upper-class types who ignored each other. The Charles Stewart seemed like it would be a lot more fun. Take the muscleman with long flowing locks sitting over by the window. Straight out of a Harlequin romance novel, her mother's favorite choice of reading material. And over there, in the opposite corner, the button-down guy sitting straight as a pencil. He reminded her of the cartoon stick figures in those little flipbooks she used to make as a fifth grader. Suppose when he was in a hurry his legs jerked up and down the same way? And the wide open face on the red-headed guy by the window was so inviting she almost walked over and introduced herself then and there. She bet he had one of those infectious laughs that made everyone else in the room smile despite themselves.

She took a sip of coffee, strong and black, and considered the women in the room. Dismiss the Americans in their boring color-coordinated outfits and the remaining females were fodder for all sorts of snarky comment and conversation. Cindy could imagine the fun her sorority sisters back in college would have had with them. The chunky one sitting close to the entryway; had she no idea of how big she looked in that get-up? Miniskirts were for teenagers, which she hadn't been for a long time. And pink leather? My god! The poor woman was clueless. Too bad Sue Ellen wasn't here. She'd gather up the dyed auburn hair, helpless make-up, hopeless outfit, and turn the sow's ear into a silk purse. And the micro-girl with the streaked blond hair. How many piercings and tattoos did you need to make your statement to the world? She didn't look old enough to dress herself. What that poor mite needed was a good hot meal and some TLC.

Wait a minute. Where did that come from? Shades of her mother. The sudden vision of her mother, settled and complacent in her over-furnished nest of a home, paging through the latest movie magazine as she lolled on her flowered chintz sofa, gave Cindy the quivers. Nope, not going to happen, not to this gal, she thought. I am destined for bigger and better things. That's why I'm here, right?

The plump black-haired girl serving eggs and sausage to the rowdy Italian teenagers at the center table looked tired. Dark circles ringed her eyes, giving her the startled look of a raccoon caught in the sudden glare of a back porch light. Cindy watched her maneuver the room with caution as she carried steaming plates of food from the kitchen and then returned, arms laden with dirty dishes and cups, weaving wide hips and thighs with care between table edges. Cindy empathized, running a hand down her thigh where she'd rammed it into the corner of the desk in her narrow room the day before. That was a bruise she could embroider some tales around when she got back home to Georgia.

And when would that be? No telling. Only two days here in Dublin and already she felt at home. Despite the traffic, the crowded sidewalks, the sirens blasting day and night, she was at ease in a way she never was in tiny Thomaston, Georgia. People were friendly here. Not that they weren't in Thomaston, but this was different. Cindy enjoyed the open readiness to talk, to share the joy of sunny days after a dark, rainy winter, the pride in their voices as they spoke of their city, their Dublin. Best of all, no one asked uncomfortable probing questions, trying to find out why she, a young woman in her late twenties – and not too hard on the eyes, she reminded herself – was here by herself, no man on her arm or by her side. They accepted her, allowed her to be; there was no judgment or critique.

Coming here was a good decision. This could be the place to begin her search for a new self and new home. Why not? That girl in front of Trinity College who cornered her yesterday about Amnesty International was from Iowa and seemed happy enough here. Iowa? South Georgia? Same difference, right? Conservative, rural, we've always done it this way and always will, don't you be the one to rock the boat, Nowheresville and Everywheresville, USA.

She had plenty of time. Only the end of May and she didn't have to tell the principal anything final for another month. They'd be able to find her replacement easy enough. Bet that smart aleck of a student teacher she had this spring would jump at the chance. He just knew he could do a better job than her any day of the week. Let him take over and see what a year of hyperactive second graders did for his ego. It would serve him right. Wipe that nose. Tie those laces. Keep them quiet --- "two-inch voices, please, children" --- and in line on the way to the potty. Bet he wouldn't be so quick to criticize once he'd been in the line of fire for a year. Little ones sap the energy right out of you. Look at her. Six years of teaching and she felt a hundred years old.

But she had to be honest with herself. She liked the teaching. And it wasn't the children or the town or the people. It was her. Much as she tried, she couldn't crawl out of that deep dark pit into the sunlight again. She thought moving back to Thomaston would help. Be closer to home, have family around her, settle into the familiar once more. Big mistake. All it did was make the memories more painful. Luke. The baby. Every place she turned, there they were, in the faces of everyone around her, pretending that all was well when it wasn't. She was living a lie.

Bo Jenkins was the final straw. After that night, she knew that she had to get out. She only agreed to the date with him because she was so lonely. Her Saturday nights had become a ritual of hopelessness, she and a bowl of microwave popcorn, watching the latest movie from Netflix on her cheap flat-screen t.v. When Bo called, she said yes before she could think twice about it. She pushed aside her doubts, the memories of all the bad dates with good-old boys that she could tally from her past. Not that Bo was a bad guy. On the contrary, he was a sweet, kind, good-natured man that any girl with common sense would consider a catch. He showed up on her doorstep, clean shaven, in fresh khakis and a white button-down shirt, skin bronzed from days spent outdoors at the farm. He'd even knocked the dirt off his boots and run his Ford F150 through the car wash. Give the fella an A for effort, she told herself.

"How about something to eat at the steak house and then a beer at Retrievers?" Bo asked her, his eyes bright with anticipation at the thought of a 12-ounce ribeye, baked potato loaded with butter and sour cream, and a draft of ice-cold Bud to wash it all down.

Cindy agreed. It beat the Lean Cuisine and cheap red wine waiting at home. By seven o'clock, when Bo pulled into the driveway, she was having second thoughts. Too late. She answered the door and let Bo escort her to the truck, thanking him for opening the door and giving her a boost with his arm as she crawled up the step to the seat of the truck. She caught the heel of her stilettos in the mud grate and cursed herself for wearing the expensive designer shoes. But Bo was a nice tall 6'2" guy who could handle a 5'8" woman in two-inch heels and Cindy had jumped at the chance. She adjusted the skirt of her new low-cut dress, another concession to her desire for escape from the routine of teaching small fry in a small town. Her mother's voice rang in her ears. "If you'd only try, honey, I just know it will get better." Well, Cindy was trying.

Bo cranked the motor and the latest Alan Jackson song blasted out of the radio, the heavy back beat sending pulses like shock waves through the air. Bo notched up the air conditioner, threw the truck in reverse, and the big F150 bounded down the driveway, spewing gravel in all directions. Alan was drifting down the Chatahoochee on a hot summer day.

"Great song, eh?" Bo yelled across the seat.

Cindy nodded and smiled, wrapping her arms across her chest. She realized that the thin polyester dress was no match for the cold air streaming out of the air conditioner. She might as well have worn a bra and panties and left it at that. So much for making a fashion statement. They headed across town to the steakhouse, Alan giving way to Josh Turner and the long black train, his deep bass voice rumbling along with the big truck's tires. Over dinner, Bo told her about his farm and his dream of buying more land, raising some feeder cattle, expanding his operation to include canola. Cindy talked about teaching, the children, her desire to be a writer someday.

They tried. But by the end of the evening, both were silent, doing their best to pretend that they were enjoying themselves. Much as they shared, born and raised in the same small Georgia town, they had almost nothing in common now. Bo's world was farming, hunting, fishing, and sports. He never read a book. The only music he listened to was country and western. He'd never been out of the county and didn't know Austria from Australia. The years in Atlanta with Luke had changed Cindy. Her world of literature, music, art, and philosophy was as foreign to Bo as his world of tractors, crop yields, guns, and fishing gear was to her. He was a good man, Cindy knew, but not for her. She said good night and closed the apartment door with relief. Her reflection nodded at her from the mirror in the hall. Cindy nodded back. "Now I know for sure. I'm too old to settle and too young to settle down." She booked her ticket to Dublin the next day.

"You finished?"

The dark-haired waitress stood at Cindy's elbow, right hand outstretched towards the plate from Cindy's breakfast. Cindy looked up into the round face and deep-sunken eyes. Who was this girl, anyway? What was going on in her life that left such dark pits under those beautiful onyx eyes? The girl bounced nervously on her toes, waiting for a reply.

"Sure, yeah. You can take it. Thank you."

Cindy smiled. The girl smiled back. Cindy watched her balance the plate on the stack cradled in her left arm. She gave Cindy another quick smile and turned towards the kitchen. Cindy thought, note to self; next time, I need to find out her name and where she's from.

Talk about eyes. Cindy rubbed her own eyes, which burned from lack of sleep. The band at the pub last night had been exceptionally good. Two guys with guitars, another with a bodhrán. They sang and played until midnight. The Band of Moonlight Love. Quite a name. Someone at the bar told her the band had a regular Wednesday night gig there at O'Shea's. The tables filled up early, that was for sure. She'd been lucky to get a stool at the bar. She'd recognized a couple of people from the night before at The Celt, especially that good-looking one with the dark hair. Wonder who he was? It was one o'clock by the time she reached the Charles Stewart and the extra pint of Guinness she'd bought to carry her through the last set was taking its toll. She remembered clutching the edge of the reception desk with one hand, concentrating on her balance while asking for her key.

"Room 101."

The cute crop-haired guy behind the desk smiled with a broad grin. "You like Dublin?" he asked in a thick eastern-European accent.

"Very much," Cindy replied, enunciating each syllable with care, left hand extended for the key. He laid the key in her palm and grinned again.

"Me, too. Especially the beer."

Cindy made her way with care, watching her feet as she descended the gradual ramp that led to the ground-floor rooms. She counted the doors on her right. She'd been fooled the first day when she looked for her room, assuming that the first door would be Room 100 and the next one Room 101 and spent a frustrating few moments trying to jam the key into the door lock before she looked up to read the bronze letters on the door. WC. She wondered how many others made that mistake. There probably was a standing bet among the staff, kind of like the football pools at home.

Here it was, Room 101. Cindy stopped, set her purse and umbrella on the floor, and put the key in the lock. She knew why they put the damned key on a suitcase-sized key ring but it made opening the lock a super-sized hassle. She had to stoop over and hold the heavy double-bound tag with her left hand while with her right she inserted the large metal key in the lock and turned it to release the dead bolt. She cursed under her breath. How many turns did it take to unlock the fucking thing anyway? "Watch your language, young lady!" her mother's voice scolded in her head. Whoops. Guess she'd had more to drink than she realized.

Finally. She pushed open the heavy wooden door and entered the compact room. Bless Ioana. She'd left the window open after she'd cleaned the room. Last night the small space had been a sauna. Cindy had made a point this morning of asking the handsome young desk clerk --- he was from Holland no less --- about the maid service and he'd given her directions to Ioana's room, # 108½, down the hall from her own #101. Cindy was a great believer in going to the source. Have a problem? Find out who manages that and talk to them. Bingo. Problem solved.

Ioana was sweet. They'd hit it off right away. Cindy admired the Romanian girl's gumption and courage in leaving her home, coming to this foreign land to work when she barely spoke the language and had no friends or family to help her. It was one thing to come here as a tourist, Cindy thought, knowing that she could go home, return to her job and her apartment, pick up her life where she left off. What must it be like to come here knowing that you had to make a go of it, that there was no return because you'd burned your bridges, you had no backup, no Plan B? Cindy knew that she could learn a lot from Ioana, if Ioana would allow it.

The combination of Guinness and five-hour time change worked their chemistry and Cindy went to sleep as soon as she hit the bed. Then, a sudden sound brought her upright, peering around the dark room. What was that noise? The edge of window surrounding the heavy blue curtains was still dark. Who was talking down the hall at the reception desk? A late arrival? Cindy punched the face of her iPhone. 5:00 o'clock. Something was going on. Footsteps, doors opening and closing, low urgent voices. She pushed back the heavy coverlet holding her feet prisoner and stood up, grabbing the robe she'd thrown across the back of the desk chair before crawling into bed. Cracking the door open, she peered down the hall. Several dark-clad figures stood in front of the reception desk. The front door swung open and she caught a glimpse of something pale lying on the front stoop, two shadowy shapes outlined by the street lamps bending over and reaching down toward the figure.

Her curiosity piqued, Cindy stepped into the hall and made her way towards the front door, slippered feet scuffling along the carpet. One of the figures straightened and turned at the sound. A garda. She stopped, one hand holding her robe together at her throat. The man approached, his face dark and brooding, a frown pulling the heavy brows down over his eyes. Cindy held her breath. She stared at the dark uniform, the strange badge on its front. A sudden wash of fear swept through her body. Not again, dear Lord, not again.

"Madam, you are a resident in this hotel?" the policeman asked.

Cindy leaned against the wall, staring at him, her eyes focused on another time, another place.

"Madam. Hello. Do you speak English?" This time, he approached and touched her arm.

Cindy gasped. She shook her head, trying to rid herself of the haze that seemed to surround and smother her. Where was she?

What was happening? Why were the police here talking to her? This must be a dream, the recurring nightmare that broke her sleep into fragments of then and now. Luke. The baby. Gone. Taken from her. Police bringing the dark with them through her door. We're so sorry, ma'am. There's been an accident. Cindy moaned.

"Madam? Are you sick? Is something wrong?" The garda leaned over her, his dark face now lined with concern, his eyes searching her face.

Cindy forced herself to look at him. He reached out, touched her arm once more. She rubbed her eyes, locked again. A garda, not state patrol. Ireland, not Georgia. This was now, not then. She took a deep breath.

"Yes, I speak English. Yes, I am a resident in this hotel. No, I am not sick. I am fine." The words came out in staccato bursts, short sentences like an elementary school primer. That was all she could manage right now.

Relief softened the garda's face. He stood up and looked back toward the front door of the hotel. "I am so sorry to bother you, madam, but we have an unfortunate incident that has occurred tonight. I must ask if you could answer a few questions for me."

Cindy nodded and followed him to the small waiting area next to the reception desk. She sat on the sofa, huddled inside of her robe, staring at the desk clerk whose young face was now wide-eyed and solemn watching the garda complete their work. Cindy wanted to hug him, tell him not to worry, that it would be fine, mother him as her own mother had done with her when her world fell apart that dark night three years ago. And with that thought, Cindy knew. Her mother was right. She would be fine, everything would work out.

After breakfast, Cindy took a walk along the river, crossing at the Ha'penny Bridge and then back again over the Millennium Bridge. She loved the bridges, each different in its way, each offering another view of the river and the city. How many times she and Luke had talked about coming here, visiting the city that Luke, born and raised in the small town of Dublin, Georgia, always referred to as "the real Dublin." Luke had been right. There could never be another city like this one.

By midmorning, the long emotional night caught up with her, and Cindy headed for the little coffee shop she'd discovered the day before. Right on the river, no more than a hut surrounded by cheap aluminum tables and chairs, it was nothing special. All it offered was coffee, cookies, and a place to sit. But, Cindy thought, what more did one need? She shifted her weight in the lightweight metal chair and gazed out at the Liffey. Georgia seemed a long way away. Gone. Not lost. Left behind. Shed like the hard carapace of the seventeen-year cicada, announcing a new beginning. Replaced. Red clay hills of Georgia now soft green folds of turf flowing to the sea. Cindy smiled. No more bad beer, whining music, lyrics of longing for the good old days. Here, a longing for the yet to come, promises of soon to be. Emigrants and immigrants. She, too, was one. Yes, she decided. This was it. She and Dublin.

Girl on the Threshold

Liz Abrams-Morley

New York called at a fortuitous time, the only reason Maureen Connelly—her mates called her Mo— answered. She'd never intended to be a nanny to anyone else's children, less so twin terrors of near six who seemed by turns to be four or three then fourteen, fresh, mean-spirited, ill-mannered. But who could blame them, Mo thought much later, after she knew their days and nights, and anyway, there was the fortune of timing.

"Family's heading back to New York City, Mo, three weeks, just. That'll give you time." It was Belle who told her of the opportunity, a couple, not Irish-born but with the name O'Meera, him thinking he'd be working for the Dublin offices of *Whatever Whatever and What*, which bank or money holders Mo neither knew nor cared. He came to find a flat only to find instead he'd be turning back to New York in under a month. Needed there, she supposed, or just not needed here abouts.

Mo was in no position to ask questions.

Most folks just pick up sweaters, tea towels, maybe a pipe, some tea, some Jameson's at the Duty Free when they holiday in Ireland. Mrs. Jason O'Meera, when asked by her husband what could he bring her back from Dublin, must have looked over at Forrest and Connor.

"Bring me a nanny," she'd said. "I hear Irish girls are hard workers. Maybe a little slow, but strong. Hard workers."

When she landed at JFK airport, her new employer not by her side but up in First Class, and set her watch—a gift from her Gran, a relic—back five hours, Mo didn't expect to be setting it forward again for a year or more. She was prepared to deal with New York for one year at least. Less than six months since—a lifetime—now, out the jet window the vivid green lined the runway. A few days home for her, a business trip for The Master.

"I want ice cream," Forrest or Connor, whichever, wailing to her like she was their mam. Herself and the husband up in first class, don't you know. "I want chocolate!"

She surprised herself, the ache in her when she saw that green.

"Mom promised ice cream!" The brat wailing, cold rain slicing sideways across the airplane windows. The parents up ahead, not looking back.

Mo hated, pretty much at first sight, the narrow sidewalks of Manhattan, the way her bag bumped against strangers and no one even scowled, the hurry of the city at every crosswalk. The faces themselves seemed cross and the feet never walked, but always seemed to run.

Back in Dublin now, once the rain stopped, she strolled the broad open band of Grafton Street, tossed a coin into the open guitar case of a human statue she particularly admired.

"Don't! Germs!" Their mother's shrill tones cut across the low notes of a busker's *Hallelujah*, as a small hand—Forrest's or Connor's—reached to touch the unmoving man caught in an attitude of hurry. A reasonable enough curiosity on the part of the boy, but curiosity, Mo had learned, was unacceptable among the New York O'Meeras, and hand sanitizer was always at the ready.

She almost felt sorry for the child. She would have, had she not hated him so much.

Good thing for Mo herself that she wasn't so concerned with perfect sanitation. Mo stepped over litter. Mo traveled light. Once her three tank tops, small pile of thong panties, two sweaters and spare pair of jeans were stowed in the half wardrobe of room 213 of the Charles Stewart Guesthouse (a clean enough room, a little threadbare here and there), not much space was left anywhere for her black boots. If she kicked them off on the floor by the bed, she'd be tripping on them every time she got up to use the jacks. Still, she stood by the one thin window and stared out at the wall opposite, into the airshaft, down to the trash and pigeon shit below, and she felt expansive for the first time in months. She felt expansive knowing that Connor and Forrest, those twin terrors, and their Wannabe-Irish pure Manhattan parents were not down the hall of their Upper East Side condo, not down the hall from her similarly small room there, but were down the street at a hotel with a lift and bellhop, a flat-screen telly bigger than this entire water closet of a room, no doubt. They were, no doubt, stepping onto thick pile carpet when they reached for the in-room phone to call room service. The Master insisted on good carpet.

"Call me Jay," he'd said, that pompous papa had said when she'd first met him, as if they were going to be friends. He said it again when they landed in New York six months ago and he repeated it at regular intervals but she wanted, despite this, to curtsy and say Master whenever he opened his mouth.

She knew he'd expected a "girl" from County Cork to be obsequious; the wife had probably expected plump, a girl with downcast eyes who would never appeal to the Master. She could tell by the ice in the full-body scan stare she gave Mo that first day that she'd neither anticipated the bleached Mohawk, nor the delicate swallowtail butterfly tattooed on the muscular left shoulder that clearly intrigued the Master.

Out with "the family" on O'Connell Street, she walked a few paces ahead of the boys, not looking back, the way a young teen might walk behind parents and siblings as if to say *I don't belong to them. Don't even think it,* and she wished she could love them, or even like them, even just one of them, Connor, or Forrest. Forrest maybe. He was a bit less snide sometimes. She couldn't even look back at them, little boys who could have been so much of what her Brian would be, had he lived—had she let him live. Curious children. Curiosity in her son would be seen as a good start, proof that he was a smart one. She would never be so fussy, never so fussy at her boy.

The carpet in the guesthouse entryway—it was hardly a real lobby—would definitely be too worn for the taste of either of her employers, but Mo was quite well pleased when she returned to retrieve her key. Her own place for three whole days while Call-me-Jay took the wife and kids around a considerably more posh Dublin than she would ever see. He was going on what he called a *Roots tour* of what he called *his Motherland* though from what she could tell no New York O'Meera had lived in Ireland for centuries.

She woke on her first solitary morning to the news of the girl on the steps. That dark-haired, friendly one, Moira, told her as she brought Mo's plate of beans and two fried eggs. A little strange, Mo thought as she watched the plate lower to the table, to be served by another girl from the Counties, a girl from the looks of her age who could be Cora, though Mo's little sister wasn't half so plump and a good deal more pale than Moira.

Strange to be served but still nice to see a familiar type, someone she could ask about the flurry of footsteps and loud knocking and gruff Garda voices that had carried up and around the winding staircases and hallways, that shook Mo out of a heavy sleep that morning. She'd been dreaming Connor and Forrest and Call-me-Jay had left word at the front desk of the Charles Stewart that her services were no longer needed, but that Call-me-Jay had left, as well, enough euros for her to keep herself in Dublin, and in bangers and mash and Guinness for at least a year feeling, maybe, a little concerned for her continued discretion about that situation last fall—no dream that—in the family's massive, pristine laundry room. No dream that, indeed—the wife and brats had been at Kinder Gym or some such.

She was deep in the dream of their desertion, happy and warm, and she didn't much favor the voices that rousted her out of her bed, but she could tell something was going on, something important, so she'd pulled on her jeans, the boots, ran gelled fingers through the hair so it would stand up and tromped down to breakfast. There she found Moira, eggs and information.

When she first heard—*dead girl, blonde, angelic, drugs suspected,* she thought of that wisp of a girl she'd spotted heading for the fourth floor, a run-away she'd guessed, too many cousins who'd been and done the same not to spot the signs of another—but Moira assured Mo that the late lamented—though lamented by whom no one seemed to know—was not a guest.

It felt wrong to be savoring the eggs, the beans and sausage once she'd learned of the dead girl, a girl who could have been her youngest cousin, Kira. It felt a little wrong to be sitting at a hotel table, time enough for two cups of good tea before she had to meet the family and turn back into Nanny Maureen. It felt wrong not to think on the lost life, so she tried to picture the girl, her last moments, the feel of cold creeping into her from the marble threshold, the feel of warm seeping out of her. No doubt Call-me-Jay and his wife would be horrified to learn about the situation and hate for her to talk about D-E-A-T-H in front of Forrest and Connor. They'd spell the word as if the kids were fecking eejits and the kids would pull at her and whine until she told them the whole story. Then Call-me-Jay would insist that she get a room at their hotel and the wife would glower.

She decided to keep the dead girl to herself.

"Don't, for pity's sake, name him. Don't even decide it's a he," Belle had urged her, when she'd hugged Belle at the airport so few months ago—a zillion years ago, it felt.

Mo had only laughed. "Oh, me and little Brian here"—such a cavalier pat to her midriff—"we'll be fine in New York. Leastways, I will be. Don't expect he's going to fare so well in the new world." She'd wanted to sound tough, to feel tough enough to handle the journey, and so she'd pulled back from Belle's hard hugs and wouldn't meet her friend's anxious gray eyes.

The morning of the sirens and loud voices and footsteps in the lobby, the morning of the dead girl on the stoop of the Charles Stewart, that, for Mo, was yet another "morning after." The night hours had been spent at The Celt—the music, dancing and how many pints had she downed? She'd woken with that feel in her mouth as if she'd been gnawing on the starched white sheets of her bed or eaten one of the thin cotton towels in her room. But no, the towels, she saw as she rose, were both in the jacks, the sheets intact on her tossed bed.

How many pints and what sweet relief, her night with Brendan and Johnny, Colleen and Belle in the Celt, able to say aloud at last what it was to be in New York City with the twins, the Ice Queen herself, and Call-me-Jay.

"You've got to leave, Mo," Colleen had said. She was the one who had no idea why she'd gone in the first place.

What sweet relief to be able without fear to shout it over the sound of guitar and whistle, over the strains of *Galway Girl*, the Americans in the corner singing along loudly but not totally on key. Every pub now at least twice a night with *Galway Girl*, no doubt to charm the euros out of two tables of Americans in the corner, to keep them coming back to part with their dollars for a week on the town. Her town.

The group at The Celt, she had to admit, had looked fine, friendly, and nothing like Call-me-Jay or the Misses, but she also had to admit that her nannying months had soured her plenty on Americans.

"You got to pack up and come home with us," Colleen had said and Brendan, always ready for a brawl, asked the address in New York.

"I'll get your things for you, Mo, and won't that fecker be sorry to see me at the door asking for them."

But it was Belle who sent her hustling to the bar for one too many pints, sweet Belle who she knew, Mo did, meant to be protective, to be loving.

"What's your Ma say about all this, Mo? I can't imagine your ma" —

And when Mo came back with it — "I haven't told me mam. You know I couldn't" — it was Belle pushing her. "Why not, Mo? You got to let her help." It was because she knew Belle most of her life that she said nothing. She also knew her ma, and knew herself, and most of all Mo knew she'd crossed some kind of line when she'd stepped onto the plane for JFK airport. There was no running back to tell Ma on the boss; that was for sure.

"Just can't." She'd tried not to sound impatient with Belle and found herself hustling to the bar — "Next round's on me" — probably the round that put her over the top so her head was pounding when the pounding started on the Charles Stewart's front door.

She wondered if the girl on the steps had been old enough to have had many nights like last night, had friends enough to drink with, to tell. She wondered whether she'd been old enough to have such mornings as Mo was getting ready to have—Tylenols and cup after cup of coffee though she'd always favored tea, and still the pounding inside her skull would probably continue until noon at least.

A long shower before she headed off to meet her charges— that was what was in order, a quick towel off with the towel she hadn't eaten. The towels on the Upper East Side were thick and thirstier than she'd been last night but she'd give anything this morning to be back home with her mam, with towels thin as these in room 213.

"You said you'd find us—what was it called? Murphy's? Maureen. You said you could find it."

Gawd she hated how he enunciated it as if she were a heath. *Moor een.*

She didn't look back at her boss. She didn't look down at his boys, one attached to each of her hands. She had wanted from the start to care as little for her never-Brian as she now cared for this Connor, this Forrest.

In her lifetime, she'd not wanted much, but she'd really wanted that.

The headache that lasted well past noon as it turned out, should have been punishment enough for her good night out, Mo thought, but if she thought it, she hadn't figured on the punishment that greeted her in the hallway of the Charles Stewart soon as she returned from her outing with the bratlings. That man from the first floor, another American but one putting on as-if Irish, as if out of Masterpiece Theater from what she could see in the hall, was holding forth about the poor dead child, something about death being just death. He was speaking the way the old people in the nursing home with her Gran would talk when their roommates or toothless friends didn't appear at breakfast after being at lunch the day before, and then didn't appear at all.

The gone ones' families, scattered to the four winds, always sent flowers. The other residents shook their heads and muttered, *It was her time,* or *She's with Jesus,* or *Really? Died has she? What's for lunch?*

She understood this attitude when you crouched on the shadowed side of eighty, or watched your health ebbing away and your friends pass on, but this man, this James whatever looked way too young to Mo's eye to be talking this way, even thinking it. Sure, a touch of gray in the hair at his temples and pulling a face every time a child went by as if their whistle-pitched voices hurt his ears, but she could tell he wasn't old enough to mimic Gran's friends.

And they were rapt listening to him They listened.

She fixed her gaze on the one clad in pink. Pink all over. Flora, someone called her, or maybe Posey. She was the resident across the hall from her own room, the one who reminded Mo of the nurse at the clinic, that sterile room, the false cheer, though that nurse had had a pretty good grip—an honestly firm and warm hand over her own.

"Deep breaths, Sweetie," the nurse had said. She'd said it over and over, a chant, an incantation for the nearly departed.

Goodbye Brian, she'd thought then.

Goodbye, Brian she thought again as she turned the heavy brass key—one, two, three times—and opened the door to her room.

The room looked smaller, dingier and closer when she stepped inside. It was, for sure, smaller than the laundry room at the penthouse in Manhattan, and if this room was a haven—hers alone now—it wouldn't be so for long. She felt the air sucked out of the room as she pictured herself back on an airplane, back in steerage as Brendan had called it, sputtering. ("They put you in fecking steerage, Mo!") and she'd be back there with Connor and Forrest, no comforting visions of her own baby Brian traveling with her as she crossed the Atlantic this time.

"They shoved you into fecking steerage," Brendan had sputtered, "Encased, surrounded. Where's the freedom in any of that?"

She pictured Brendan on his silver Harley, riding free north of the Liffey. She pictured herself on the back of his Harley, his pride, her arms wrapped around her friend's waist, the damp breeze of Dublin in her ears.

On the plane, the children would be whining that they'd never found Murphy's while the Ice Queen and Call-me-Jay napped up in First Class, scented pillows over their eyes. Back in Manhattan, Call-me-Jay's well-rested eyes would be on her as soon as the Missus turned her back.

She picked up her mobile and punched in Brendan's number, praying to whatever God she could still believe in that he'd answer. She prayed he'd answer quickly.

Homeland

Sara Kay Rupnik

James came to Dublin to escape the small-minded negativity of Ohio. He came with his own expansive, anything-is-possible state of mind and told himself he could stay until something good happened. Or until he ran out of funds. Whichever came first. He told himself his life was going to change for better, and if he had to go back to Ohio without proof positive of that change, at least he would have a taste of it, a calm, clear vision of what was to come.

Now, after only two days, his confidence ebbed like Dublin Bay at low tide. He lay sprawled on the black print bedspread, still dressed in his stiff blazer, and stared at the ceiling of Room 109 while the women squawked outside his door. Every evening they gathered at that juncture of the hallways like crows – no, like *magpies* -- to feast on the crumbs of news each had gathered during their busy, busy, busy frivolous days. Tourists with too much money and too little imagination. He rolled onto his side to face the window. Dusk was falling over the parking lot – no, *car park* -- and soon it would be time for the pub. The pub and the Guinness and the good craic of being in a place where, for once in his life, he felt he belonged.

He reconsidered. Maybe after this long, disconcerting day, he should stay in. He could have a cuppa and his leftover bap from lunch. He could sit at this tiny table and watch the telly. He could play the Irishman inside the Charles Stewart as well as out, could he not?

Yesterday when James emerged from Arrivals with his plastic bin of family records, he felt a tug on his soul. A visceral reaction that made his blood thrum like a fiddle's strings. This was *his* country, land of *his* people. Their genes were his genes, and he, James Moore, true descendant of the O'Moher Clan was returning to reclaim their centuries old kinship. God almighty, the air was fresh here. He inhaled deeply, lifting his face skyward and noticing the particular blue above him, bright blue it was and studded with clouds. What a fine day. What a fine country to begin anew. James imagined he smelled the sea. Sea brine mingled with a touch of peat, no doubt about it.

Jaysus, what a grand old city! Its streets teemed with people, multi-cultural people, people seeking a new life like himself. Except he was seeking an old life, an ancient life, a promised life. In his white shirt and black blazer, James fancied himself a lawyer. No, a *solicitor*. He strode past the bullet-ridden GPO and the statues of patriots. He had never been to Dublin, and yet he knew it like the back of his hand. He had done his homework.

When checking into the Charles Stewart Guesthouse, the dark-eyed girl at reception glanced at his bin of records and reverently handed over his key. "Breakfast from 7:30 to 10." Her voice was soft, the lilt of an unknown language rolling over her tongue. James glanced at the key tag, which was the size of a wallet, and plunged down the ramped hallway toward #109. Well now. This is what Joyce – or maybe Yeats, one of them – might call "the bowels" of the building. In its original functioning state as the Georgian home of Gogarty household, this section of the guesthouse might have merely been a backyard. No, a *garden*. A carriage yard. A small patch of vacant ground.

He passed an Irish girl emerging from Room 101 and nodded in a manner he hoped would not invite conversation. He had no patience for young women and their chattering. The girl smiled at his armload of family records. "Well now," she drawled, "look at you."

Not Irish at all, but American. And a Southerner at that. James kept going, turning right at the next corner and feeling less like a solicitor with every step. Only a poet, a grim, suicidal poet, could appreciate a room so far removed from the sunshine. Although it would work well for a jet-lagged traveler, too.

James slept deeply that first afternoon, slept through the comings and goings of the other guests, and awoke in the shank of the evening feeling not only rested, but driven. He was here where he belonged, and he would make it work.   When he saw the crescent moon rise over the blossoming tree opposite the Charles Stewart, he took it as a sign.

He joined the crowds along O'Connell Street, matching their quick and purposeful strides. Again he breathed deeply, inhaling the night as he dipped in and out of side streets. Finding Moore Street, really no more than an alley, almost reduced him to tears. His street, his city, his country. He was home, for the love of God, and that alone called for a celebration.   A solitary celebration amongst his countrymen at The Celt, where the husky voice of the woman singer gave mournful a whole new meaning. The Guinness never tasted better and the music, all those tunes of love and loss, never rang so true. James watched in a mixture of wonder and pride as local men danced with tourist women, and then with each other. The little old guy in black grabbed James by the elbow and twirled him around before taking hold of a young woman in white, her hair as blonde as her shirt.

Still spinning, James lurched into the cool damp air and followed the cobblestones toward the massive silver spire at the intersection. God, what a night. Full of gratitude to be here in this place in this moment, he wanted to fall on his knees and kiss the bronzed feet of James Joyce. Instead, he righted himself and turned northward where his deep, dark bed awaited him.

That next morning James' new poetic frame of mind might have sensed tragedy in the air, but in truth, the less poetic James was hung-over and hungry, and the girl who took breakfast orders at the Charles Stewart was distracted and slow to respond. "Problem in the kitchen?" James asked.

"Not at all." She blinked. "What will ye have?" He carried juice and coffee to the table facing the emergency exit. Today, this first full day of his new life, he wanted no distractions. Today he would start with the genealogy section of the National Library, get his facts firmed up, and then move on to the Land Registry. He knew about dying intestate, unclaimed land, and squatters' rights. He had done is homework.

"Pure dead she was," announced a woman behind him. "No more than a girl, Bridget. No older than yourself."

"On the steps, you say?"

"The very steps we take every day. Our very own doorstep. 'Tis mad like."

James had no use for young girls and their fondness for soap operas. He bent over his plate of eggs and rashers, the bright wheels of broiled tomato, and contemplated the oldest Irishman on his family tree. Michael Moore, born in 1742. Why had Michael left Ireland only to fight the British on American soil and die soon after? Had too many brothers and sisters crowded the poor lad from the ancestral land?

"Drugs are not cool, man." A long-haired, muscle-bound American plopped down opposite James like a bouncer blocking the exit.

"Pardon me?" James noticed the man's plate of fruits and grains and braced himself for a lecture on the dangers of food additives.

"Man, that dead girl. That perfect little angel was a druggie."

"What dead girl?" James squinted over the top of his glasses. "What angel?"

"The one on the front steps. The dude at the front desk said she looked like an angel."

Later, off to the National Library with his plastic bin in hand, James stepped carefully, avoiding the bottom stone step of the Charles Stewart altogether. He did not want the residue of tragedy to waft his way, and he did not want to think about young girls. He was too old for young girls and too young to give up on women completely. Although he had pretty much given up. What was the point of putting himself out there, pouring out his whole heart to women who barely listened?

James was young when he brought Cara Riley to his granddad's farm, but not so young as to be ignorant of love and its power to blind and maim. He had been bruised before, dumped on his head by Stacy in high school and stabbed in the heart by Amanda in college, so he had waited to bring Cara to the Moore homestead and spill out his dreams. Even then he should have known better.

"This could be ours, someday," he told her that summer day when he pointed out the bright green field on the hillside. "Our own land to build your dream house. Would you like that, Cara?"

Cara turned her lovely head just as a cloud passed over the far sunny field and darkened it from grass green to a deep shade of moss. "That would be awesome, James."

James detested the word *awesome*, and he should have known right then and there that he and Cara and the small green field were doomed, but as she clutched her curls back from her face to smile up at him, James held on to hope. "I'm not much for the country though," she said. "Could we build somewhere near a beach instead?"

"Where in Central Ohio would we find a beach?" he had wanted to say, but James held his tongue, held on longer than anyone with half a clue until the lovely Cara found someone more *awesome* than James himself had been. A lifeguard or a surfer, James imagined.   Someone as tanned and sinewy as the American at breakfast.

Ah, Cara Riley with the Irish name and luminous skin. She had held him in the palm of her hand for quite a while before squashing him flat.   "It makes no sense for us to stay together, James," she finally told him. "We have nothing in common."

That American guy at breakfast would have a dozen girls hanging on him, James imagined as he turned into The National Library.   That guy would have his fill of yoga instructors and exercise freaks, hair stylists and fashion models, girls who cared more about their looks than their brains. Although for a superficial type, the dude seemed genuinely shook up about the dead girl. "She was a little blonde," he told James.   "Her arms bruised with needle tracks. It could have been me once upon a time. Could have been any of us."

Not me, James wanted to say. Even in the days after Cara dumped him, not once had he been desperate enough to turn to drugs. To stick a needle in his arm. And this dead girl lived here in the land of song and laughter, fairies and rainbows, poets and musicians, not in the goddamned middle of bleak, small-minded Ohio. There was no excuse for it.

James fumed as he headed back toward the Liffey, one mere mortal amidst the masses crossing Westmoreland in unison. Dublin just might be too crowded, too loud, too busy, too friendly, perhaps for its own good. He had begun to resent the well-meaning Irish who popped out at every corner to offer directions and point the way. He resented the good cheer and good causes that greeted him at every turn. Even the beggars didn't ask outright, but kneeled like supplicants over their paper cups. Like that girl sitting here along Bank of Ireland, knees drawn to her chin, blonde head bent over her hands, her cup extended. A shade of the dead girl.

He veered away. His heels loudly pounded the stones and his shoulder ached from his tight grip on his document file. As he crossed O'Connell Bridge, the sun shifted to his left, and the air rising from the river turned chill. James raised the collar of his blazer. What unpredictable temperatures. What fickle weather. What a miserable place.

"'Tis your land, James," his grandfather had promised. "You are an O'Moher, the descendent of an ancient King, my boy. The ancestral land is there for the claiming." What bullshit. His grandfather was no more than a con man, as jovial and full of advice as every other old gent James had encountered in Dublin. Barely into his forties, James felt he himself had grown as ancient as high king in the space of an afternoon.

At least the pedestrian traffic here on expansive O'Connell Street was bearable. Workers boarded busses. Tourists headed to hotels. Schoolchildren stoked on sugar surged away from James. This was better. He could breathe now. He could make these last few blocks to the Charles Stewart. He could climb those half-dozen stone steps and swing down the corridor to where the women staying on his floor would be gathering, planting themselves outside his door and ooh-ooh-oohing about the dead girl. "She's dead for Chrissakes," James would shout to them as he sidled past.

When had his instincts, his gut feeling that he was onto something good, failed him so completely?

Now that shadows from the car park filled his room, James raised one hand to turn on the bedside lamp. His stomach rumbled as he slid from the shiny spread. Yes, it was surely tea time, that vague hour when the Irish ate cold cuts and iced cakes and substituted booze for tea. He rummaged through the shelf holding the electric pot, cup and saucer, and packets of tea, sugar, and creamer. Outside his door, the women grew louder, but tonight James found their voices more feminine than avian. He could make out distinct murmurs (*what a pity*) and exclamations (*can you imagine!*) and quotations (*James Joyce said "Redheaded women buck like goats."*)

Whatever they were discussing, the Southern girl was the clearest. Or maybe just the loudest. "That American guy. He is so serious."

James agreed that the American muscle man was serious, although *intense* might be a better word choice for him. Maybe even *rigid* when it came to his foody quirks. James stood holding the empty pot and listened more closely. "That's his room," said one woman.

"I dare you," said another with an Irish accent.

When the knock came, James startled, and then reacted impulsively. He flung open the door without stopping to set down the pot, smooth out his bed-rumpled clothes, or straighten his glasses. He opened the door so quickly, the women also startled, recoiling collectively, but not completely taking flight.

"We were just wondering," said the Southern girl.

"Yes?" Why would they seek his advice? Why, in this guesthouse of desperate seekers, would they recognize him as the voice of good, Midwestern practical experience? His eyes flitted over them. Well, maybe the younger ones, the one with the platinum Mohawk or the skinny one with the tattooed neck, might give him a listen. He'd been known to command an audience when he led a sales meeting. But the others, the one with the black-flowered bag, the Southern Belle, and the big-busted one, they would turn right back on him faster than a swallow of the black stuff. He kept his grip on the doorknob. "Wondering what?"

The Southern Belle's smile appeared genuine. "Have you heard anything new about the girl on the steps?"

Here was his chance to say let the dead be dead, but instead, James glanced down at the empty pot, the electrical cord dangling to his knees, and allowed the frustration, the complete and utter discouragement of his day to mute him.

"You heard there was a girl found dead on the steps this morning?" This from the woman in pink.

He nodded, trying to shake off that moment when the Irish genealogist, polite, but steadfast, completely failed to grasp the importance of James' mission. "I've come all the way from the States to be told you have no record of my family?" James was incredulous.

"I have no record of your family's ties to the O'Moher Clan, but we have other Moores that may be of interest to you. Scots-Irish, they would be. And Anglo-Irish." The man looked hopeful, which only incited James further.

"My Moores were pure Irish." James sputtered in retreat. "Not British."

Now these women were regarding him with that same pathetically hopeful expression, and James suddenly found himself holding forth on the fleetingness of life and how, like it or not, one's choices sealed one's fate. "The fate of that poor girl" -- he threw in "poor" solely to gain the sympathy of his audience – "was simply the result of too many bad choices. She chose the wrong friends, the wrong love, the wrong dream." He shrugged. "Dreams are our downfall."

It was obvious these women had made some bad choices as well, James noticed. Too much peroxide, too many piercings, and the too eager-to-please expression on the Southern Belle. Then there was the unfortunate one dressed in pink. Not a girl at all, but a woman past thirty who must know her skirt was too short and her hair an ungodly shade of red. Yet, something about her wistful expression, her yearning eyes, intrigued him.

She recognized him, he imagined. She knew at once James was not descended from an ancient king, but simply the ineffectual manager of the Tractor Supply Company in Guernsey, Ohio. This woman also knew all about poor choices. She knew what it was to lose the love of her life. Or to mistake beauty for true emotion. To follow a ridiculous notion born of passion. And yet, she carried it off, ridiculous or not.

James had gone by Moore Street on his way back from the library. Purely for the hell of it. Purely to see his family name in black and white. Instead of the shuttered alleyway of the previous night, he found the narrow street bustling with street vendors selling everything from vegetables and flowers to electronics. Stalls filled the cobblestones while the buildings on Moore Street housed shops and cafes of every ethnicity. His street had come to life! At the corner, James paused to see his street sign and then saw the second sign. Here on this very spot under his feet where Moore Street met Parnell Street, Padraig Pearce had surrendered to English forces in 1916.

The leaders of the Irish Rebellion had surrendered. They had surrendered and were executed, and yet Ireland went on to become a free state. The apparent fruitlessness of that long ago moment on Moore Street sank into his bones.

James took a closer look at the women gathered before him. Obviously they did not judge one another on appearances. These women wore their imperfections like high fashion, exaggerating what lesser women might conceal. There was something to be said for such honesty, he supposed, and more to be said for their interest in him, the non-muscled American also following an unlikely dream.

"You know," James said grandly, "my Irish grandfather believed no life should go un-mourned. What say we head to a pub to wake the dead girl?"

"You're not Irish." The pierced waif's tone was scornful.

"Ah, but I am." He let go of the doorknob to skim his palm over his bristly scalp. He didn't mind their attention in the slightest. They were in Dublin, for the love of God. His wallet was not yet empty, and the night was young. *He* was young. And free. For tonight, at least, he was here in his homeland and anything might happen.

The Soul of a Poet

Mary Coley

Flora "Posey" Mulvane used a paper clip to pin the red drapes shut over the tiny window of her fourth floor room at Dublin's Charles Stewart Guesthouse, but the bloody summer sun still charged through. In despair, she kicked at the flimsy wood desk, then let herself fall onto the board-hard double bed that filled three-fourths of the minimal room.

It wasn't the best of digs for her long-awaited week in Dublin, but it was the best she could do on her salary. She had scrimped and saved, and saved and scrimped. For fifteen years, ever since her sixteenth birthday, she'd been saving, both for this trip and the other thing, that big event girls dream about. She glanced at the small calendar she had thumb-tacked to the wall. Seven days. That was all the time she had to find him.

"Better pass boldly into that other world, in the full glory of some passion, than fade and wither dismally with age." So here she was, just as the famous James Joyce had suggested, passing boldly. She had to at least try, before she went on to wither.

Flora ran her fingers through her uneven bob, feeling the once-brown hair now turned to a brilliant red and wondered if she'd made a mistake with the color. She had wanted a special look for this trip, something that would draw the attention of the other soul who must surely be on a quest identical to her own. Her mum had hated the hair color, but Keith had smiled his usual smile and said, "Brilliant. Absolutely brilliant. That's my Posey-girl. Expect the unexpected."

He was kind to her, and this was how she repaid him, with a last minute quest for her soul mate? She might as well have spit in his face.

Her gaze focused on the single globe light centered in the white ceiling and she reached for her I-pod. The room filled with her favorite Irish dirge, "Brian Boru's March." In her mind a mist rose and filled the room with grayness that overwhelmed the shards of sun piercing the crack between the draperies.

For a moment, optimism dampened the desperation that had filled her mind for the past several weeks. The clock was ticking.

A few of her favorite lines from W. B. Yeats popped into her mind. "The trees are in their autumn beauty, The woodland paths are dry, Under the October twilight the water Mirrors a still sky." No, it wasn't the right season, but it was a lovely thought from a lovely poet – a man with a sensitive, intelligent mind, a man with soft hands and eyes that smoldered with unknown passions? Surely such men still existed. She had staked her future on it.

Yesterday she'd taken the bus from Limerick all the way to the poetic center of Dublin. Surely her soul mate was here in this hotel. At check-in Sunday night, as she waited alone in the tiny foyer of the Charles Stewart Guesthouse, she had scanned the crowd. One of these people *must* embody the spirit she sought so fervently, otherwise why would the Charles Stewart have been the only north central Dublin guesthouse with an available room? Best of all, it was just around the corner from the Writer's Museum on Parnell Square. Surely, if the soul of an Irish poet- the soul she loved so much – now inhabited another body on Earth, it would return here, wouldn't it?

She'd chosen to wear a pink leather mini skirt, black leather jacket and black textured hose under black boots as well as a pink and white scarf. She carried her large white duffel decorated with pink flowers. The most important things she owned were in that duffel; her poetry books, her contact lens solutions and packets, her iPod and her makeup.

Last night Flora had searched the faces of the strangers who would share the boarding house with her for at least one night.

Initially, she was intrigued by the tall gentleman. American. Quiet, reserved. But then he glanced around the small entryway and she saw no poetic spirit, no creative bend. His eyes didn't smolder behind his glasses when his look flitted her way.

And the Fabio-type - the man with the buff body and long flowing hair - was obviously too self-centered and too obsessed with appearances to be her poet.

But then, her eyes met those of a short, plump woman with black hair and such white skin. The woman scanned the crowd with fiery eyes and then hurried up the wide carpeted front stairs. Her black pants and white shirt along with the pail she carried, identified her as a maid. But just for that second, during the woman's speedy scan of the crowd, Flora saw a hint of something. She drew in her breath.

Who was to say that the poet's soul she was seeking didn't live now in the body of a woman?

Her survey of the rest of the guesthouse inhabitants before check-in didn't yield any more possible soul mates. She climbed four flights of stairs to her room and fell into a dreamless slumber.

The next morning, Gardai swarmed all over the sidewalk in front of the Charles Stewart and more sirens blasted their way down the street so that even Flora, from her rear closet of a room on the fourth floor, grabbed her pink-flowered duffel and rushed down the hallway, practically flying over the stairs and past reception as she made her way to the front stoop.

The horrified public stared, fisted hands tight against their mouths, at the dead girl on the bottom step.

Breathless, Flora chewed at her knuckles as she jockeyed for a spot in the watching crowd. *Oh, my.* Her heart ceased to beat.

The blonde hair, the blue dress, and thin fragile arms, bruised. Sightless eyes staring up. Flora shifted, eased past another onlooker to get closer. She blinked, and blinked again.

Was it Aida? Her little sister Aida? What was she doing here?!

She closed her eyes and tried to stop the fluttering of her heart. Then, Flora's look flickered over the crowd before returning to that perfect face. *So like Aida.* Her eyes moved quickly, shifting constantly, looking beyond what was really there.

Had Keith sent her?

Flora pressed one flattened palm to her chest. *It could not be Aida. She was imagining things.*

The man, the American who stood next to her on the stoop, sighed deeply. "Tragic," he said as he lifted a hand to check the straightness of his collar and push his glasses up on his nose.

A whisper moved among the crowd. Drugs? A Beating? Suicide?

Flora hugged her flowered duffel close to her body and a moan slipped out. *Aida, Aida. Did you follow me here?* A swell of salty tears slipped over her bottom eyelid.

"Anyone know this woman?" A garda called. One by one the heads of the gathered crowd shook 'no.' The crowd began to disperse. Flora continued to stare at the frail body. She needed some proof. *Aida, or not Aida?*

A hand touched her shoulder and Flora looked at the athletic girl, her across-the-hall neighbor, her pierced eyebrow only inches away. A streak of bright red - her own new color - screamed from the girl's auburn hair. "What happened? Did they say?"

Flora shrugged and dropped her look as she turned away, avoiding any chance that she would have to endure the tattoo on the girl's neck, the nose ring, the heavy deep purple eye shadow that offended her country sensibility. *This girl didn't know Aida. She didn't know anything.*

But the girl persisted. "I like your hair. It's grand, the color is."

Flora stopped, turned back and searched the girl's eyes. *No poet there. Only curiosity.*

She pushed past the another trim young girl in the doorway, the one with the spiky bleached Mohawk. Butterfly tattoo on her left shoulder, pierced eyebrow, and nose studs on this one. Her poet was not enclosed in these youngsters. But the second girl's eyes widened as she took in Flora's hair, her jacket, mini skirt, boots and stockings. The girl's fierce look eased as the muscles of her mouth formed a smile. Flora saw shrewdness there, an unexpected intelligence hiding behind the keen eyes. But still, no soul of a poet.

Flora moved into the building, away from any chance of an unnecessary entanglement. Friends weren't worth the time to make here in Dublin. Her holiday was short, only a week, and then back to Limerick, her wedding and the small animal emergency hospital.

She tripped over the threshold by reception and the long-haired conceit grabbed her elbow and pulled her upright.

"Easy there," he cooed at her. Even white teeth flashed in a ready smile.

She allowed herself to meet his gaze and then returned his smile before she hurried down the hallway to the dining room for breakfast.

The room buzzed with half-truths about the dead girl on the step.

She wanted to scream but instead bit her lower lip and ricocheted out of balance between the tables to finally sink into a corner chair. She dropped her duffel into the empty seat next to her but kept her arm looped through the handle.

"Are you all right?"

It was the pale-skinned plump girl, the maid with the dreamy eyes. Flora wanted to pull her close and peer into those eyes to see if she had a poet's soul, but the room was full of people.

"I said, are you all right? You look a little sick. The dead girl, I'm guessing. You saw her."

Flora closed her eyes. "Yes." She could hardly say the word.

"Bloody awful, that. Let me get you some coffee. And a full breakfast?" The woman bounced on the soles of her feet, hovering over the end of the table.

"Not sure I can eat anything," Flora said. In fact, she was sure that she couldn't. Her stomach twisted and questions roared in her mind. She kept coming back to the thin girl on the step. It couldn't be her sister. *What was Aida doing here? And how could she be dead?*

The lovely girl brought her a cup of coffee, gave her shoulder a pat and then moved to another table.

The tables emptied and filled again and still Flora sat sipping her coffee, letting the girl refill it for her even though she was supposed to serve herself. Flora's body felt heavy, too heavy to move. She closed her eyes and saw the girl's dead body. She opened her eyes and heard the voices, saying the same things over and over. "What do you suppose happened?"

Flora didn't know. But she suspected. She suspected that Aida got wind of her plan to come to Dublin, and came to 'talk some sense into her' as Da so often said. Guilt pounded on her temples. She had to know.

Back in her room, she made a quick phone call to the clinic. Aida was indeed grooming and walking the dogs just as Flora had paid her in advance to do. *Aida was safe.* Flora laid on the board-hard bed and stared at the ceiling fixture.

The sun stabbed its way through the slit in the curtains. She rolled over and closed her eyes. *Blast the sun. Where was the cloudy rainy day that she so needed?* The pain that seeing the thin young woman dead on the front stoop had evoked in her heart had temporarily distracted her from her purpose. She would not be able to find the poet's soul on a busy bright day.

On the evening of the third day, Flora left the fifth pub she'd inhabited that afternoon, all of them known to have been frequented by at least one person on the list of Dublin literary geniuses. A quote from Brendan Behan drove her today, "The most important things to do in the world are to get something to eat, something to drink and somebody to love you."

She felt as if she was floating above her body. She'd only had a pint of Guinness at each pub, pacing herself, but the brew had left her woozy, in spite of the bowls of peanuts the barkeeps had kindly provided. She'd spent the hours peering down into the creamy foam, then peering up into the eyes of the pub patrons as they passed. Her eyes ached with seeking.

Halfway up O'Connell Street, she found an empty seat. The edge of the cement bench cut into her upper thigh, so Flora pulled at her pink leather mini skirt, stretching it over the rough edge. She performed the act without letting her eyes stray from their purpose. She peered into the face of each passerby, watching for that glint of recognition, that spark of light cutting through the gray misty air as his soul searched for hers.

But then, the mist dissolved and the sun beamed down. Horrified she bowed her head. The luminosity was lost in the sunlight. How could she ever find that soul when human eyes reflected the daylight and made any inner light invisible? And likewise, how could his soul see her own inner light?

The pink in her outfit contrasting with her black accessories were all she had to draw him to her - and she feared that would not be enough in strong sun. "And there I asked beneath a lonely cloud Of strange delight, with one bird singing loud . . ." the lines from J.M. Synge's poem came to her, along with a tear. Flora glanced up one last time as she stood, intending to make her way back to the Guesthouse to enclose herself in her room until either the clouds and mist returned or night fell.

Their eyes met. A spark of recognition.

Because of his sly smile, Flora knew the spark for what it was. Some human pheromone - not 'the soul' she was looking for. Just a temporary diversion. She did not have time. This week in Dublin was 'do or die.' Her wedding in Limerick and her return to work at the Animal Hospital loomed.

She smoothed her pink skirt, broke eye contact with the man, and stumbled on the curb as she crossed the street. She was too old for one night stands but too young yet for 'til death do us part.

Flora got caught at the light on O'Connell Street at the River Liffey. People crushed around her and she began to slide into despair. Time was flitting away and she was no closer to finding the one she searched for than she had been when she arrived. Flora still held on to the hope that it was someone at the Guesthouse, someone perhaps who had not yet checked in.

She hurried up the street and was almost to the front stoop, when she stopped. The man - young, clean cut, handsome and obviously already drunk - was speaking to everyone who waited for the bus at the stop in front of the Charles Stewart. He was too young to be such a drunk, she thought, and too old for anyone to excuse his behavior.

He turned toward her, the sun dipped behind a cloud, and his eyes shone with an inward light. In that instant, when their eyes met - him, drunk to dull his despair - Flora had expected to swell with hope and joy and finally, oh, finally, an end to longing.

Instead she thought of Keith, steady, ruddy-cheeked farmer. He indulged her moods and longings and patiently patted her shoulder and stroked just below her jawbone when he wanted her to look up at him. He'd be at the Limerick Station on Sunday to welcome her home, to hills, to bogs and stony walls. He'd stand and wait as people poured from the bus, seeking a flash of pink leather or a bob of red hair. She pictured his face, his green eyes, as the last of the passengers climbed down the steps and sauntered away down the sidewalk.

"Where's my Posey?" he'd ask. He'd leap the metal steps up into the bus and have a look for himself. The empty bus. His sturdy, thick hands would lift to smooth his thinning hair and stroke his beard. *Oh, Keith.*

Flora paused on the step and the man stopped flapping his arms at those waiting for the bus. His eyes drilled into hers. Electric, magnetic, celestial pull. Moon, sun, sea drawing at her altogether.

The man stumbled as he made the two steps across the crowded walk, and caught himself on the wrought-iron railing. He swayed toward her. "Wanna go for a pint?" And then, she was sure that he said, under his breath, a famous quote from Brendan Behan, "One drink is too many for me, and a thousand not enough."

She clutched the flowered duffel to her bosom as the breath whooshed out of her.

Nights on the farm, staring up at the stars, Keith's fingers entwined with hers, she'd imagined the emotion of this moment. She smiled. When the handsome young man extended his arm, she slipped her hand into the crook of it and let him lead her back down the street toward the pubs. She didn't care where they went, she only cared that she had found someone with that inner light - a light that was sure to reveal a poetic soul. At last!

Ten days later:
A silent church.
A silent man at the altar, head bowed.

The light rain whispers against the shimmering leaded windows.

The ancient oak door creaks only once as it opens, but the sound is enough for Keith. He raises his head.

Flora stands in the doorway, her pink veil floating in a cloud around her.

One last time, to be certain, she peers down the aisle and sees, like the lights of a bus forging ahead through a dense fog, Keith's piercing gaze.

Her heart swells. And to think, she'd almost given Keith up for a drunken bloke who didn't know or care to know a single line of poetry.

Contributors

Liz Abrams-Morley's collection, *Necessary Turns*, was published by Word Press in 2010 and won an Eric Hoffer Award for Excellence in Small Press Publishing that year. Other collections include *Learning to Calculate the Half Life* (Zinka Press, 2001,) and *What Winter Reveals* (Plan B Press, 2005). Her poems and short stories have been published in a variety of nationally distributed anthologies, journals and ezines, and have been read on NPR. New poems are in *Persimmon Tree, Philadelphia Stories* and *Passager*. Co-founder and co-director of *Around the Block Writing Collaborative*, Liz is on the MFA faculty of Rosemont College and works with Philadelphia Public Schools' children in literacy through arts programs. Wife, mother, grandma, teacher, neighbor, sister, friend—Liz wades knee deep in the flow of everyday life from which she draws both inspiration and, occasionally, exasperation.

Mary Coley lives in Tulsa, Oklahoma. Her at-home family consists of her husband, Daryl, and two dogs, Gunner and Annie. A lifelong writer and nature lover, Mary currently authors a nature blog hosted on her website, and is actively fine-tuning and marketing seven book-length manuscripts as well as dozens of short stories. She is a member of The Society of Children's Book Writers and Illustrators and the Oklahoma Writers Federation, as well as numerous non-profit nature organizations. Her nonfiction book, Environmentalism: How You Can Make A Difference, was published by Capstone Press in 2009.

Jeanne Goldberg-Leopold has always loved to write. She has been a member of various writing groups and she runs a writing club for teenage girls. She especially enjoys writing for young adults. She also likes writing about baseball and is an avid Phillies fan.

MaryAnn L. Miller's debut book of poems, *Locus Mentis*, has been published by PS Books of Philadelphia Stories magazine. She was Resident Book Artist at the Experimental Printmaking Institute, Lafayette College since 2001. Her work is in the National Museum of Women in the Arts and other special collections. She has been a contributing writer on the arts for Garden State Woman magazine and the International Review of African American Art. Most recently, Miller is involved in a Postgraduate Semester at Vermont College of Fine Arts working with the poet David Wojahn. She is the founder of Lucia Press publishing hand bound fine artists' books in limited editions.

Tracy Robert, a born and reared Californian, relocated briefly to South Carolina but is now back in the Golden State. A co-founder of Around the Block Writers Collaborative, she holds an MFA in writing, and has 25 years of experience teaching all levels of writing, plus publications in periodicals and anthologies, most notably *Forever Sisters* (**Pocket Books,** 1999). Her yet-to-be published novella, *Flashcards*, won the Pirate's Alley Faulkner Award for Literature. An excerpt from another novella, *The Curse of Ambrosia*, appears in the anthology, *When Last on the Mountain* (Holy Cow! Press, 2010).

Sara Kay Rupnik lives in Richmond, Virginia, Coastal Georgia, and West Cork, Ireland. She holds a M.F.A. in Writing from Vermont College and is co-founder of Around the Block Writers Collaborative. Her fiction, nominated for a Pushcart Prize and short-listed for the 2010 Sean O'Faolain Short Story Prize, appears in literary journals from the U.S. and the U.K.

Andy Sachar expected always to make his living as a writer, and, in fact, was rather productive in his early years. However, he spent too much time in college and ad agencies, and became a beach bum by mistake. Years of waste, wondrous adventures, and procrastination followed, but Andy captured none of it in print. And then one day, after a string of unlikely events, he suddenly found himself President and General Manager of DCNA, a Delaware corporation with warehouses throughout the United States. There was only one way out.

Nancy W. Shumaker lives in Statesboro, Georgia. A retired Spanish professor and director of international studies at Georgia Southern University, she now oversees development of the University's service learning programs. Nancy is an active member of her local Altrusa and Rotary clubs. An avid reader, Nancy is using her retirement as an opportunity to expand her own creative writing activities.

Kathleen Worrell is a retired university grant writer living in deep East Texas. She has poems in *Spiky Palm, Hurricane Blues: Katrina and Rita,* and *Future Cycle.* Her short story, *Adios, Lash Larue* appeared in *Buffalo Carp.* In 2009 she received honorable mention in the Chautauqua Literary Journal contest for her poem, *On Cezanne's Apples*, and in 2010, second place in the Nacogdoches Writers Guild for the poem *Texas Two-step into Spring.*

Around the Block Writers Collaborative works with writers from everywhere. Founded by Liz Abrams-Morley, Tracy Robert, and Sara Kay Rupnik, who are published writers, professional teachers, and longtime friends, Around the Block offers a variety of writing services. In addition to Fall and Spring Semesters via email, Summer and Winter Workshops are held in lovely, intriguing places. Like Dublin. For upcoming events, consult the website: www.aroundtheblockwriters.org

www.ingramcontent.com/pod-product-compliance
Lightning Source LLC
Chambersburg PA
CBHW031856170626
46807CB00004B/1760